MEDUSA
of the
ROSES

MEDUSA
of the
ROSES

A NOVEL **Navid Sinaki**

Grove Press
New York

FIRST EDITION

Printed in the United States of America

First Grove Atlantic hardcover edition: August 2024

Library of Congress Cataloging-in-Publication data
is available for this title.

ISBN 978-0-8021-6303-5
eISBN 978-0-8021-6304-2

Grove Press
an imprint of Grove Atlantic
154 West 14th Street
New York, NY 10011

Distributed by Publishers Group West

groveatlantic.com

24 25 26 27   10 9 8 7 6 5 4 3 2 1

To Luis C. for the chapters

MEDUSA

of the

ROSES

1

Tiresias was mine. I always played the part of the man from Greek mythology who turned into a woman simply by striking two snakes.

It would have made the most sense if we pretended to be Zal and Rudabeh, even though we were two boys. Zal, who I always loved more than a friend, shared his name with a fabled Persian prince. And like Rudabeh, I was told my hair could pass for snakes. But I chose Tiresias when we played in a garden where gravity was especially cruel. Since our house was built on a slant, cherries from a neighbor's tree rolled into our yard from one side and out the other before we could catch the fruit. Pomegranate trees kicked up rocks in search of water that was always out of reach. Nectarines didn't just fall, they were impaled by stones. If ever one fell on my head, I'd pretend I deserved it in preparation for juices I'd eventually catch on my neck.

Sometimes I wore a veil for the role. A simple lace tablecloth completed my metamorphosis. In the myth, Tiresias eventually struck another two snakes and returned from being a woman to being a man, so we looked for the fruit vendor who hammered his cantaloupes at the end of the day. He would rather they rot than go for free. He also sold oranges I peeled to see what it felt like to walk around with foreskin, as I assumed they did in ancient Greece.

"It's hard to love you," Zal began to say when we were older. Not because I was a boy who wore veils and a fake foreskin. "Because you're so infatuated with death."

Perhaps he was right. I was the boy who gathered moths for spiders' webs. I would polish the light bulbs when a memorial was strung for a kid who had drowned. I'd cry at spring because, with the dry leaves gone, for months nobody would talk about death.

Zal, let our words be a ribbon between the mouths of painted angels. If I start a conversation with you and keep it to myself, at least that won't end.

2

I've long since mastered the disappearing act. Every time you leave, I take our photos off the refrigerator, even though I leave the evil-eye magnets. None of our pictures—postcard-style ones you took of places we fucked—are explicit to outsiders. The caravanserai near Nushabad. You pointed your camera outward while I was still splayed. The bird garden in Lavizan where I gave you head. Curious cranes tried not to look. And in Orost, we stood at the travertines of Badab-e Surt. You photographed the puddles on the rock layers while I dried myself with the cum rag we brought along.

I empty the frames and shove our photos in the box that once held a samovar. Whenever you leave, I cut off the top inch of each candle so no burn marks remain. Even though the tapers slowly shrink from being sawed, I appreciate the ceremony to make it all brand-new when I am rid of you.

I don't clear out your shirts from the closet. If I was more superstitious, perhaps setting fire to the sleeves might force you to combust wherever you are, whether you're driving or back where you live. I'd rather set your dress shirt on the mattress and whisper where your ears would be. I'd proclaim that it's over. Is it over?

I take out the VHSes you bought for me in an act of pettiness. Erasing some of the videos requires me to hold down the record button on the VCR while playing a channel that's all static.

"Videos are easier to smuggle," you swore, since most airport guards didn't have a VHS player handy like they did for DVDs. My VCR is decades old. Holding down the record button is a challenge. I sometimes let go and see a scrap of the film—Jean Harlow on a telephone. Gheysar's dance. Mary Pickford as she faints. Should I have just suggested a long weekend instead of a murder? Maybe you never expected me to give in, to really want to leave.

Because you left again without a goodbye, I need help to sleep. A heavy pillow over my eyes usually does the trick. Not now. I picture the man swinging from a citron tree, for no reason other than being found with a man. We read about it in the morning paper. He was someone like us, though we didn't know him.

"They claim he was caught with an underaged boy," I said earlier today.

"A lie. Anything to kill a faggot. The same old charge for each new cast."

"I don't want our lives to end the same way." The words weren't enough to get you to act. Maybe a dramatic gesture would rile you up. I shook the paper hoping some dust would catch on your eyes to force a tear or two.

"We're safe."

I wasn't so sure. Out of panic, I would always check our curtains to make certain they'd been shut tight. The air conditioner, ready to rat us out, causes the curtains to part. I'm convinced people live downstairs, though I never see anyone else. I might catch a dustbin left outside before entering, but never do I hear voices or footsteps or conversations. The apartment is my uncle's. He's gone for most of the year, so you and I have a safe place to fuck and fight.

We aren't lovers in Antarctica who have to swear off summer fruit in order to hold hands. Here, one does not date, one mates for life. If by chance a man meets another and the two share more than words, Rumi mixtapes, a book by Kerouac, what generous luck. Otherwise it is a marriage arranged in fear of death. Death shares our bed because I had the misfortune of being fortunate, of finding love so early. Now I only dread its end.

I mentioned the newspaper article. We argued. You knocked the samovar over on your way out. I picked up the gold kettle knowing I'd burn my hands.

The cat that knows when I'm alone. Black with black eyes, fur on only half its tail. It paces when you are gone to remind me I am loveless again. How the stray gets to our balcony, I never know. It circles my legs.

I hope you'll come back to continue the conversation you wanted me to lead. About your wife. About a gun under the bridge, her pearls in the bathtub, as little blood as possible. A clean escape, a new life in another place without fear of an executioner. It was a joke. Maybe it wasn't.

I take a third pill. I close my eyes and, finally, sleep comes.

I wake up hungover on the bedroom balcony. I never sleep outside, but I was desperate enough for any change. The phone rings inside. I hurry into the apartment before any of our invisible neighbors can complain. The room sways. There's a mess. I smell the smoke of your cigarettes. You came back while I was knocked out. Maybe you didn't realize I was pill-drunk and asleep outside. Did you sneak into the apartment alone to make sure the coast was clear?

I try to make sense of the scene you've only recently left behind. Two cups. A shoe with burgundy laces.

I answer the phone, ready to scold you. "Hello?" Even my voice is dizzy.

"Are you related to Zal?" a woman asks.

"Yes." Our lie.

"He was attacked," the nurse says.

A haunted lamp distracts me. Even with the light switched off, the bulb still buzzes with electricity. I blame the ghosts. They want me to see what you've left behind.

"You got that, sir?"

The nurse doesn't stop chewing her gum. Machines levitate past the phone. Or maybe the nurse is walking, hence the intercoms and passing screams; a murmur of Arabic, immigrants in the ER; the opening and closing of filing cabinets. Some of them derail from rust, the way the nurse keeps pulling out a drawer and pushing it back in.

"Don't come with a full stomach," she says. "We have enough to do without cleaning another mess."

I grab a coat from the closet. It's something for me to do, even though I won't need a layer during this heat wave. I make sure the stove is off, though I haven't used it in days. I need the safety of routine to buy me time, some crevice to help me process. I look around for something to toss. I feel I should. I pause to finally make sense of the scene. Two cups. A condom wrapper. You were here with someone else.

3

I can't remember how to speak when I call for a cab, but I somehow make it into one. The driver forces small talk. Weather. Politics. Street closures.

"Allah be with you," he says at the end. I don't remember how to respond. He tells me the fare. I don't understand numbers. I hold open my wallet. A smile obscures his face. Later I realize he's taken too much.

I can't rush to your side like the king from Attar's *The Conference of the Birds*, who raced his messenger to see who could get to his ailing beloved first. How could I explain to anyone else who you are to me? It's as difficult as when we were kids, when I'd beg your aunt to let you come out to play.

"Where are you taking him?" she'd ask.

I didn't take you anywhere. You would run out the door and grab my hand, and take me up and up and up to the end of our steep street, until we had no place else but down. You carried me along because I understood you. I knew you were too afraid to own anything feminine, so you pretended spoons were dolls and tore off your shirt buttons just to have an excuse to sew.

The hospital's automatic doors open and close whenever a crow passes by. One in particular mistakes a prune for a cockroach. The crow nears the entrance. The door opens. Afraid, the bird flies back. The hospital gift shop is full of kids. They rearrange the cards, all Get Well. Half of them have stock photos of cats. Roses, irises, dry bouquets. The new batch comes in tomorrow. I don't buy anything. You don't deserve a reward.

The hospital workers mumble among themselves. Children from the cancer wing string together paper flowers to pass the time. A young girl in a gray scarf walks with a basket of tissue pansies. A little boy with mismatched socks does his best to straighten a paper daisy without tearing off a petal. Some kids curl their garland around a bulletin board, but don't fasten it with pins. When they leave, the sway of a passing wheelchair knocks it down. I pull an old tack from the bulletin board to fasten the garland.

I keep stalling. Paper garlands have found their way onto the doorframe of the men's bathroom. When we were teens, I wished there was a spy hole in the urinal whenever I would hear you unbuckling your belt. I would get too hard to piss. Couldn't I just give your armpit a lick? I wanted to ask. I munched my shirt collar to keep calm.

I wash my hands four times. I can't think of anything else to do. At the wrist some of my skin loosens.

I finally go to the front desk and ask for you by name.
"He's this way," a nurse says.

She doesn't ask how I know you. She doesn't care, just wants to hurry me in to hurry you out to hurry the next person in so she can continue an accelerated speed. A woman paces in the waiting room, sweat pooling on her upper lip. Though her eyebrows are black, her faint mustache is blonde. The nurse gestures to her.

"This lady called the ambulance."

I nod a greeting, not a thank-you.

She wipes the sweat off her forehead. As soon as she sees me, she leaps up to go. "I just wanted to make sure someone came for him."

"Wait. Please. What happened?"

She drops her arms. I can sense her defeat. She hoped to leave without giving any sordid details.

"These men. They were attacking them."

"Them?"

"Yes." She looks around. She's scared somehow with one conversation she'll forever be tied to me. "He was with some young man. And these hooligans started to attack."

"You stopped them?"

With a look, she begs me to leave her out of it.

"I just wanted to make sure someone came for him. That's all."

I could thank her for making sure you made it here alive. Just as easily, I could curse her for building the image in my mind. Some young man. Not me.

She leaves the empty waiting room. It must have been busier earlier. Folding chairs are scattered in almost comical randomness. One even faces the wall. Part of me expects to see him. The young man probably watches from outside the building hoping the coast will clear for his own visit.

I unwrap a box of rose hard candies from the gift shop while I wait for him. I place one on my tongue. The taste reminds me of visiting my grandmother's village. Sweeping muck away from the rose coffers. I take two more candies. They don't disintegrate. I can't produce enough spit. Instead three harden into one. But why not add another? You fucked someone else. He was probably better and looser and kinder than me. But the fact that you might want to run away with him, that you might die with someone else but me—that, not the final rose candy I shove into my already full mouth, that thought makes me heave. At that betrayal, at that sting, I produce more than enough spit. I vomit nothingness and everything. All the sweets you ever made for me, rice cookies and baklava pearled with pistachios, and walnut honey cakes, and blueberries, blueness, fountains of milk and cum, all yours.

It should have been us facing each other with blood from our mouths reaching for a kiss, until our bodies, kicked to pulp, inched closer and closer.

You're in the ward with all the people who are trying their damnedest to keep from oozing outside of themselves. They hold their holes shut, or seal their lips, or wrap themselves tight so nothing falls out, an intestine, a fetus, a third eye.

In your room, no flowers. Nobody has come to see you yet. The young man, the one who was holding your hand, would he have brought you lilacs? Would he have bought a wreath and buried it in your neck? He'd hurry in. He'd lick your chin.

"Is it over?" the young man would ask, referring to your love for me.

You'd nod. You two would be set. But, without me, it wouldn't be the same. You need adultery to feel like an adult.

You don't open your eyes. You're plugged in to so many tubes and twisty straws widen your nose. Your face is stapled, covered in plates. You keep me up with your beeps and gurgles. They rush you in. They rush you out. I get up to go home.

"That's all right," a doctor says. "You can stay."

I'm relieved he doesn't oust me from your room. He turns a corner before I finish reading judgment on his face.

Your blue shirt sits on the chair next to your hospital bed, cut in two, now purple from all the blood. I bought it for you. You probably didn't choke him. He probably didn't need to be goaded into getting fucked. I used to always hesitate. And even though I tried to prepare by using thin glasses of blackberry syrup or gardenia shampoo bottles or even the back of a spatula, I still flinch when you get ready to fuck me. My fear is that I'm dirty. My ass, sure, even after cleaning it as best as I can. But also, my preference. With him, you probably don't hear the slight mumble of apology. I prefer when you force me before I have a chance to protest.

A nurse breaks my trance. She enters with a clear, un-labeled bag and shoves your shirt inside. There's no senti-mentality to the act.

"It's all yours." She plops it on my lap. "You should get outta here. Go for a walk. Grab a soda. Do something to make yourself feel whole. Even just for a minute."

Look here at the beggar I am, asking the colors of your old clothes to come back. Through the bag I can tell the col-lar is stiff, like when we danced our only dance in a public place. A waltz, years ago. I'm not sure how I knew the steps. A wedding. Yours. The cake was rotten, but I didn't want to complain. Instead we hid in the hallway that separated the men and the women, the hallway from which we heard the women cheer the bride, and the men call out for you. Some-where between their two CD players—traditional folk music in one room, Donna Summer in the other—I put my head on your shoulder. In the space between the two rooms, you led the dance.

They wheel you in. A moment of unplanned eye contact. I turn away. It's much easier to look at the walls than see something in your eyes I don't want to see. A look of panic that it's me here, not him. I scan the room again. Near your hospital bed they have your teeth arranged in a vial, some powdered to halves. I've never seen them out of place. To keep from fainting—your wide-open mouth drooling blood improvisations down your neck—I hold your teeth up to the window. Lit from behind, the molars glow. Outside the window a bee is stuck. I tap the glass to get it to move. It doesn't. I tap slightly harder. The bee falls down dead.

The doctors leave the room. To be alone with you now is the most heinous thing of all. Before I can curse or cry, I find I'm already standing over your bed. My mouth is already on yours. I kiss you once, perhaps twice. You with no teeth, except for one. Your stubborn wisdom tooth.

Your teeth are more sensitive than the rest of you. I'm sure it's because of me. I craved pomegranates when we were kids, so you would bite into their tough skins and tear out openings just for me. More than once I confused the pomegranate juice down your chin for blood from your teeth.

"I'm fine." You always lie during dessert. You eat ice cream often, no matter the pain.

Does he know about that ache, that I was the cause of it? Did he choke on any of your teeth? You share an intimacy with him I'll never know.

Perhaps because of him, you never planned on leaving with me. My suggestion was extreme, our circumstances too much to overcome. To be with you here, in our home city, seemed unlikely.

"We can pretend you're blind," you said once. "That way you can take my hand for hours."

We tested this hypothesis. I closed my eyes to see where you'd take me. I kept my eyes closed to memorize how you walked, the quick step forward, the sudden stops to let anyone pass before us. My sunglasses were too tight. We bought them from a man on the sidewalk who also sold burnt corn. Anything quick to try your experiment. We could finally be lovers in public. I only had to sacrifice my sight.

With my eyes closed I noticed how much you apologized to strangers. Was it a show for me? You graciously stopped to let anyone pass, but you wouldn't let go of my hand. And the thought, the eclipse: What could I sacrifice to keep you with me?

You fall asleep in your hospital bed before we have a chance to speak. They've stitched your cheek. After the first kick to your head, one of your teeth got stuck in your mouth. By the next kick, it cut directly through your face. They've widened your smile, my love. When you come to, they pump you with painkillers. But there's a minute when you can feel. In that minute, you get out as many tears as you can before you drift off again.

"Can you give me any information about him?" I ask a nurse. "About the other guy?"

She shakes her head. A doctor joins her, this one with a safety pin holding her scarf over her scrubs. They whisper to each other.

"The other young man?" the doctor says.

"Do you know his name? I have to see him."

"Sorry. We can't help."

I feel the beginning stages of an obsession, wanting to see if his hair is thick where mine will thin. You and I have been alive for longer, together enough to witness every detail of each other's bodies. If a corner starts to sag, or a gray pube furrows through, we'd notice. Did you betray me out of boredom? It used to be easy to keep your attention—back when we were still acting out our firsts.

Our first kiss. You admitted to stealing a metronome.

"Why?" I asked.

"To put under my bed." To fake my heartbeat while you slept.

You were embarrassed by the sentiment. It's how I knew you were earnest. To recover, you became cruel. You called me a wicked boy.

You said, "A bitch like you could even bruise milk."

Later, I sat in front of my grandmother's vanity to align my lips with a mauve stain on the mirror. There, I wished to be your bitch bride. I wanted to see myself how you saw me. At times sweetly. At times with aggression. You were right. I had a strange power. Apricots would bruise before I touched them.

I need to do something, to make myself whole, just like the nurse suggested. She's onto me. Pretty soon, she might realize why I care about you so much.

I want to ruin the lives of all other lovers. I want to take the smoke out of the mouths of strangers to taste the burn meant for air. The only way we'll be even is if I fuck someone else. There's a balance to the thought, a balance between us I'd like to find.

4

"If you were a woman, we could get married," you once said. "It'd be different if you were my wife."

The voice comes to me, a ribbon, always with a hark I never speak aloud. I can't keep the thought out of my mind, though. It begins a stampede. Perhaps if I were a woman, I would know how to keep a man. The thought is arbitrary enough to stay.

I barely have enough gas to drive to the sculpture garden, the third stall in the southernmost bathroom. It's the hour of parables. There's no use being coy while waiting for routine sidelong glances. As I walk under the one bulb, the bathroom light hisses from cream to yellow. I turn my head away from the drain where the shit stink creeps up eager for a companion. I douse rose water behind my ear. I can betray you too. I clean myself with the bathroom hose. There's a little shame afterward when a few drops slosh about in my jeans. An optimistic act, not unlike asking for grace.

I wait to see if anyone else will join. To get hard I try recalling porn clips, wide-open jockstraps, oiled holes and POVs where the men blink too much waiting for the money

17

shot. It's a lie to say I've thought only about you. But nothing on my phone starts more than a slight erection. At least hard, if anyone comes in and sees me jacking off, he can either join the happening side by side or drop down to his knees.

I haven't jacked off in so long, I can feel the cum curdling in me. I'm sure I'll spew fully formed statues: Ceres and Minerva, Vidar and Odin. I'll convulse out clumps of eyes and mouths from mythological busts. Zorvan and Atar, Fuxi and Nuwa.

The thought of you and him. That does it for me.

A man enters after I finish myself off. He grunts when he sees me, surprised anyone else is in there too. It's late. Must be a janitor. I try to start again, but quickly lose interest in myself.

Was your young man trying to be funny? Leaving with just one shoe because he had no need for another? Back in the apartment, I near it without touching. True, you might have found a guy who is new to love, but I can find one whose jaw drops when I show him what I can do with my throat. Even if he's younger than us, that novelty will wear off. Everything joins antiquity.

I imagine my rival returning to apologize. I'd invite him up. He'd put on his shoe. I'd pour us tea from my broken samovar. When I kicked its side in, did it happen just as they were kicking your face? I play both scenes together. My foot in the samovar. A boot in your cheek. I wince.

I remember our fight that day.

"I'm ready to leave," I said before you disappeared. Before I cut the tapers. Before I knew about him. When I thought your wife was my only real rival.

You paused before reacting, hesitant to believe me.

"Where?"

"Isfahan."

"Not farther?"

"I can't. Not while my mother's alive."

There's something finite about going too far. My grandmother wouldn't have wanted me to go at all. That much I knew. After having lost one of her children too young, and her son to another continent, she'd have wanted me to look after my mom.

You shook your head.

"You don't believe me?" I asked.

There was almost a laugh. "You're the one who always made me wait."

"Not anymore. Not with the panic of death."

"And for money?"

"You have to trust me."

"Of course I do."

You said it without thinking, but there was a change in your breathing. Your palms were sweaty, though you never admit your uneasiness. I saw how discreetly you tried to wipe them on your back pockets. Never discreet enough.

"You're serious?" you asked.

"Serious as a citron tree."

The room was blue. I didn't have the nerve to change the video, to play Barbara Stanwyck's ploy over again. I'd gotten out of it what I needed. The wrong time flickered on the screen. Maybe the machine thought we were elsewhere. Bangalore. Bangkok. Budapest. Blue roses on the tables and cum stains on the sheets I always try to soften with no luck.

You wavered. Yes, there were the perfunctory answers of "I shouldn't" or "It's not possible" or "You must be joking," but you eventually settled on the question I was hoping for.

"How?" We were both excited by the thought. "It's a pretty big leap. Death."

"Is it?" For a moment we both considered how close it was to being over at any moment. With a poisoned kiss, a string of pearls pulled tight, or a stumble off a balcony. Your wife would be gone and we would be free.

"Who will miss her?" I asked.

Your demeanor changed quickly, as if a hypnotist snapped his fingers cities away. You faced the window. "You've backed out before. You're a coward when it comes to me."

A harsh accusation. "Being with you is the least cowardly thing I've ever done. I'm ready now. I won't back out."

You still weren't convinced. "Will all the violence be worth it?"

"Define violence. There will be cruelty regardless, whether or not we control it."

Your next sigh was especially deep, went on for what felt like minutes. "Sometimes I just want to start over."

"Exactly. Me too."

"With someone else. There's too much history with you."

I sit with my tea. I'll let the boy in when he comes. He'll put on his shoe. We'll sit over cups of tea in place of an hourglass. Once the tea joins the coldness of the room, once the steam stops its ascension, the young man will leave. And I'll be here waiting for the hospital to release you. When we die, I want to be together. I want to be at your side either as the cause or as the witness.

5

I make a stop on my way to work. The laces are an easy enough place to begin. If I knew anything else, if I knew any other detail about what he looked like and what he ate, his diet and his fetishes, then maybe I would start there. I'm uneasy with the thought that some young man knows about me and I know nothing about him.

"We don't carry those laces," a store owner says. The fifth shop I've tried. "He probably dyed them himself with sumac. You need some? We have so much in the back. My daughter says it's good for Alzheimer's. I told her I have sorry luck. I've never forgotten a thing."

The shopkeeper is right. The dye on the laces is uneven. I go back to the apartment and try three different mixtures to get the exact color. The sun dries them quickly. I hang them out the window where they drip red tears down the building.

I drag myself to work. I easily convinced my uncle to give me a job at his hotel. He felt guilty for leaving my mom, his sister, behind in Iran.

"I guess it's the least I can do," he said, same as when he gave me the keys to the apartment he hasn't used since he moved to the U.S.

"How generous of him," you said of the arrangement. When he sent me money to repaint the walls, I used it to buy us a samovar for the guests we never have.

"Impeccable," my uncle declared on his next visit of what he thought was a fresh coat of white. I had pocketed the extra money and bought new light bulbs for his lamps. The added brightness did the trick.

At least in the hotel I can fake normalcy until you're well. Down the corridors I push carts with luggage, or racks to replace towels. I turn down beds, empty the trash, but I always leave a little trace that someone was there. The tiniest bit of foil in the trash can. A pube in the shower. Or I tear the corner of a tea bag, which will make patrons decide to boil coffee instead.

When cleaning the rooms, I simply open the drawers and see what the rich visitors, often the wealthiest ones to traipse through Tehran, have snuck by customs. It's easier to steal drugs from them, since no one will report pillaged pharmaceuticals for fear of being arrested. And undershirts are such trivial things. Men usually think they've misplaced them.

A guest on the sixth floor forgot to shut her door completely. When I realize the room is empty, I size up what's in each drawer. A gaudy ring sits on a crumpled blouse.

The door opens. The occupant enters her room crying and stops when she catches me. She drops a Pomeranian with a bow that matches her Chanel scarf. I remove her ring.

"What do you think you're doing?" the woman asks. She peels lint from her lipstick. Her dog is too scared to approach.

I play it like it's no big deal.

"Cleaning. Like you asked." I gesture to the placard outside of the door. A lie for every trap. "Maybe you meant to use the *Do Not Disturb* side? Not the *Please Clean*?"

"I never put anything on the door." She doubts herself. Her dog shuffles to the bathroom.

"Then maybe it was a joke. We'll have to check the cameras to see which guest it was. Probably some bored children."

She looks down at the jewel I have in my hands.

"I was placing it in the room safe," I say before she can interrogate me. "I figured you'd want to keep it guarded. Whether or not it's real."

This hits a nerve. "It certainly is!"

Outside the door, I hear her yelling at the concierge. Once she's off the phone, she starts crying again. Her sobs make me wish I had more common responses to betrayal. A burn, a bruise, or a cut I can point to as proof I'm dividing from myself.

There is a certain ridiculousness to our ritual of meeting at my uncle's hotel. We always ended up in the corner room on the twelfth floor, a room slightly smaller than the rest. It's never occupied since the sink makes noises on its own. Guests complain that it's haunted, but I keep it clean for us.

And if anyone ever hears us when we're fuck drunk, it only confirms their suspicions that the room is filthy with ghosts.

"Better to be safe," my uncle said when I told him about the complaints over the phone.

He had me buy four Korans for the bedside table.

We would arrive in secret. First you, and later me when off the clock, after ducking from any of the chambermaids or bellboys on their phones.

Days before our planned meetings, I'd always come to stock the mini fridge we had long emptied of bottles. And I'd tighten the bedsheets under the mattress, and clean the mirror again as I would in any other room.

You loved the generic painting on the wall, a copy of a copy of a Matisse with persimmons. You wanted it for our apartment as if it were a prop. You also wanted a duplicate of the room's VCR, and the marble minibar, and the dressers. It was a cruel joke at first. I laughed when you took a photo of the painting on the wall, the copy of a copy. And when you had a print of it framed, I laughed and pointed out the glare. You didn't choose an angle that hid the sconce in the background. Its reflection on the glass made its way under the glass of our frame.

"Good," you said when I pointed it out. To you, it wasn't a joke. It was a brutal imperfection. The same kind you see in us—a catastrophe you can't resist.

The hotel rooms are quiet except for the last mutterings of the people who've just left. I swear I can hear our old dialogues too, and all the other sentences we would have spoken if we lived together for longer than spare weekends, days tucked away like the dates tucked away by your diabetic aunt.

I lie on the thirteenth floor and try to listen to our room from above. Part of me imagines the young man, Sumac, stumbling into this hotel to lie on our bed. His young breath would sweeten the sheets.

Eventually I work up the nerve to check our secret room for any other clues you've left. Another condom. Glassware. The missing shoe with dusty red laces. Anything. I stand as far to the corner as possible. I start at the periphery and circle the walls so I can catch any detail of the room that might be askew, any sign you were here. I'm disappointed to see there is no new evidence. I stare at a pathetic plastic bag in the wastebasket that carried fruit we've already eaten. The bookshelf is missing my favorites.

When I was six, my mother brought me a book of classical mythology the library had forgotten to trash. She couldn't find children's books on Persian folktales, so she settled on one with Greek beasts and deities. It came with 3D glasses to bring the illustrations to life, to help me see Pegasus fly, or where exactly Cassiopeia ended up in the night sky, or to sit at the mast of Odysseus's ship.

"This will do until I find one about our histories," my mother said. At first I thought she meant the myths within our family, since she swore tragedies happened in threes. Three house fires. Three suicides. Two tragic weddings, which she joked about.

"Make sure it becomes three." Her challenge to me.

When I started to learn about Persian lore, I adjusted the book. I'd set out my jewel tone markers to adapt the myths. Pegasus became Rakhsh, Rostam's steed. I only had to change his eyes. Almond-shaped always made things look more Persian. I drew feathers to turn his skin from white to rose. The Sphinx that badgered Oedipus easily became a simurgh. I had a knack for drawing fire. But Tiresias was the figure who haunted me most.

I realize our hotel room isn't the same. Something's wrong. The glass door to the balcony is open all the way, instead of just a tiny bit to air out the dead skin of our past fucks. The screen door is mangled from the outside, the large thing folded over itself and pulled off the rails. Someone must have entered our room from the balcony, even though no objects seem to be missing. The building across from the hotel winks as ceiling fans make the dingy drapes sway.

6

Maybe you left proof in the car. Maybe a piece of paper fell out of your pocket.

The hotel parking lot is empty. Most tourists avoid going outside. It's too hot and the residue from sweat instantly crystallizes on sunglasses. Tongues are immediately dried of their spit. Even eyelashes bend backward to close eyes tight. The way some guests walk, I can tell the heat twists their pubes inward.

The other men I work with have tweezed eyebrows far more delicate than any woman I've ever met. And at night, after the fifth call to prayer, their blue vape lights signal where they stand in the parking lot, arguing over which one's girlfriend looks best without her hijab. They swap phones for proof.

"Anjir," one of them calls out to me. "You married yet?"

"No," another one jokes. "He's too shy."

"Tell me, how many conversations can sparrows have?" A reference to the poetry of Attar, which I've probably revisited too much. "You're always reading or listening to cassettes." Not streaming EDM beats like the rest of them, for which they've bought T-shirts that strobe along with the music of mediocre DJs pretending they're in Ibiza. "Now that's real music," they say, in comparison to my tapes: Baudelaire dictations in Arabic, Aslani cassettes.

I lock my car after a fruitless search. "Is that all?" I ask. One of them shakes a tab in a Ziploc bag.

"You want in?" He caught me watching him swim once. It was only because nobody told him the pool was closed. The pipes were overstuffed with rats that finally turned the water pink. He winks at me.

"I'm good."

He rushes toward me and pins me to a wall. He fakes a punch to my gut. I don't push back. I like the intimacy, even at its most violent. He's disappointed when I smile instead of flinching.

I watch the hotel guests with the help of mirrored alcoves, niches, and doorways. Through the sheets of glass, I can easily see all the lobby rooms, the main entryway, and the elongated halls leading to the east or north wings. Above the cartouches of scenes from various European coronations, there are at least four of Rostam's labors carved into the relief. In one, he wields his sword in the face of ornate dragons.

A woman with apricot lips sits in the lobby. She wears bangles on both wrists, and a scarf with a subtle golden thread. She's there when I enter the changing room. She's there when I exit dressed for work in white gloves and black slacks, a dress shirt and black shoes. I'm hesitant to interact with her, not even a hello. I have no interest in meeting someone new. That requires piling on euphemisms and redacting truths. I hate waiting for strangers to ask why I'm not married.

Panj, one of the chambermaids, pulls me to the kitchen within the kitchen, the room typically gurgling with saffron butter and nettle soup. It's cleared out for the night, but she already has a kettle boiling. Another reading. I once helped her calculate the numerology of her birth month with some equation I made up on the spot.

"The Vizier is looking for you," Panj says. She moves a frozen wedding cake left out to thaw.

It's an ongoing joke. Even though my uncle owns the hotel, there's a more experienced manager, one who doesn't drink or disappear or read instead of cleaning the gold-plated restaurant toilets. We call him the Vizier because of how quickly he snitches to my uncle. Panj sits with me in the kitchen and transfers music from one candy-colored phone to another. She laughed when I asked why she chose the number panj for her nickname.

"Because of my five abortions."

She prefers a nickname to the one she was born with (Fereshteh), signaling a holiness she doesn't care to carry. She's nice to me because she knows I can read tea leaves. My gift, my grandmother's gift. Panj discovered it by accident. She saw the way I turned a teacup out of habit.

"It's not like you can see anything in there, right?"

Truth was that I did. In the hotel kitchen, Panj prepares a demitasse of Turkish coffee.

"Sweetheart, you really didn't know?" she asks after I tell her vague details about your infidelity. "You didn't read about the affair in Earl Grey?" I shake my head. "What a shame. If I had your gift, I'd carry around a thermos of tea so I could read into everyone's everything. Strangers on the street, bankers, and manicurists, just to make sure they won't take too much off the cuticle."

Neighbors would line up around my grandmother's courtyard, past the pepper trees at her entryway, just to have their fortunes read. The busiest time was usually around the new year. Gussied-up women in freshly ironed scarves would arrive and ask for any hint of what the future held.

"Tell us anything at all, azizam." She hated when they called her dearest.

There were few variations to her readings. Typically, she gave her audiences simple messages about their children doing well on exams, their husbands excelling in business, and they themselves finding some sort of happiness. When they left, though, my grandma would tell me the truth.

"Her husband is a straying cat. Her child will sip too much moon. And she herself will be tempted to leap." She spoke in metaphors rather than discuss adultery, alcoholism, and suicide outright.

At some point, I turned a cup and saw symbols in it too. But we had a pact: She didn't look in my teacups, and I tried my best not to look in hers. Perhaps at an early age she saw roses surround my name, or hyacinths that when not around Nowruz might have signaled my taste for other men. But we would wrap the cord of the electric samovar and tuck it away before my mother spotted what she was doing.

"She hasn't forgiven me," my grandma said while we quickly hid the samovar, even if the kettle was still full of boiling water. I would start her sewing machine by pressing the pedal so the sound could be heard from the street. I didn't know until later which tragedy my mom couldn't forget.

"Look here." My grandma pointed to the coralline stains at the bottom of a teacup. "If you're stuck during a reading, you can always look for animals or flora."

The Primordial Bull of Ahura Mazda. A sacred feather from the Huma bird. The Sasanian prince Khusraw spying on his love.

I used to secretly read the dregs in your afternoon tea to make sure our futures were aligned. A hat. A column. A field of horizontal trees. Our first kiss.

Panj usually covers her mouth around hotel guests because of her dead tooth, one gray alongside tame whites. She's not self-conscious around me though.

"Why do you care so much about your fortune?" I ask her.

"A girl needs any help she can get. Call it one asshole too many."

A bellboy interrupts our conversation. He sticks his head into the kitchen and points at me.

"The Vizier is looking for you."

"Five minutes," Panj says. She checks the time on her phone with a jelly-scented case. "I want to meet someone tonight." She hands me a few bills to bribe her way to a better fortune. "What's he gonna look like?" I turn the cup over. "Wait!" She turns off the kitchen lights for the ceremony. "That's better now, isn't it?"

It doesn't change what I see. An owl, a stem, an overturned snake.

"He'll look like whatever you want him to look like." A generic response to bring her joy.

"I knew it! I might as well read my own fortune. It says I'm divine too, doesn't it?"

At the bottom of the cup where most of the coffee has settled, I lick my finger and make a circle. A big drip. A sedentary tear. Panj turns off the stove. She doesn't need to hear any more. In a matter of seconds, the water stops steaming.

"You really didn't know she'd break your heart?" she asks again. I don't tell her the truth, about your cut-open cheek, that we're two men.

"No. I didn't see a thing."

"That girl's an idiot." She finishes drawing a beauty mark on her cheek. It takes her three tries to get it right. "You should always have them drink a cup of tea." But all love ends the same way. Weight on the lap, one lover leaves the other when dead. "I'd cover a table with tea in all the china I own. One by one, I'd make him drink it—whomever I might consider for a husband. And after he left, I'd read each one to make sure he's worth it. A mug to read about his finances, a teacup to make sure his mom is dead. I'd make him drink a full bowl so I could judge the sex." She takes her coffee back. "Maybe I'm gifted too," she continues. She turns her cup. "Yes, yes. I see a man." Her voice lowers in performance. "He's tall and he has a thin wallet because he only pays with large bills. Here, I see a diagonal stripe on his tie and a coat over his arm. Yes, yes. This man will do." She nods like it's my fortune she's telling.

Another person peeks into the kitchen. Panj's sister, who works in the laundry facility.

"You're bothering the fortune teller again? Ask him if I'll get into college."

Panj laughs. "College is for decent girls, you bitch."

We burn wild rue to cover the smell of weed. The smoke reminds me of your aunt who out of superstition burned esfand over our heads to keep us safe from some nondescript calamity to come.

I wait in the kitchen alone until the rue finishes giving off smoke.

Panj peeks her head back into the kitchen. "You coming?"

I nod to the herb that hasn't fully stopped smoking.

"It's bad luck to leave before it finishes."

She laughs. "Can it get any worse?"

7

Will Sumac dare to show his face at your bedside? I should be there, documenting your recovery. Instead, I'm back in the hotel lobby.

"You've obviously heard the rumor," the Vizier says at the front desk. He nods to the woman with apricot lips. "You want to know her secret?" He hopes I'll perk up, that I'll be excited by the gossip.

"Not really."

Since I'm uninterested, he changes the subject. "Your uncle wants the photos."

"Again? Already?"

My uncle requests daily photos of various spots in the hotel, a scavenger hunt around the place to make sure it's clean. The laundry annex and the electric boxes and the ladle holder in the serving room. He's always looking for reasons to fire me. He usually visits in winter just to have an excuse to not leave his own hotel.

"It's far too cold to go elsewhere."

My task then is to dust the snow off the roses. Even the gardeners aren't asked to work outside like I am. They only have to keep the rooftop pool clean, though prospective Olympians practice indoors for the season. But laboring around roses isn't new. I used to drive a five-hour-long route to Qamsar to help my grandma with similar chores for weeks on end. It began as a punishment but eventually became a routine I continued until my grandmother's death.

My mother never understood why I obsessed over roses, even though she was the one who told me that roses were snakes under a spell.

"If you look under the petals, there are teeth," my mother said.

A dead rose could be an easy snake to crack in two. My father complained, not because I was a boy collecting flowers—he didn't mind.

"But Tehran's roses look best when alive," he said. "Not like the hyacinths of Tabriz, or the lotuses of Lalezar."

I knew the roses would die anyway. At least gray, they became endless. In my apartment closet, gray roses perfume my dead grandmother's wigs.

"I heard a guest caught you wearing her rings," the Vizier says. "How would your uncle feel about that?" He laughs at his perverse taunt.

"You don't have it in you."

"True. I wouldn't hurt you. Not on purpose."

The woman with the apricot lips appears behind him. "My good man," she says. "Leave the young one alone. He gives the rest of us something good to look at."

Her lips are so large, I imagine myself falling in. I nod in gratitude at her attempt to compliment me. She smiles and returns to her seat in the lobby. She's still there when I finish watering the planters and go up to another floor. She's there when I come back down with half-eaten room service trays. I pick up a glass of tea from the kitchen. The restaurant staff gestures to the lobby.

"That woman," a server with prim eyebrows says. "She's ordered several cups. She's waiting for one delivered by you."

I'm sure she's just another stranger on the prowl for a confidant. I set down her cup of tea, and with it a bowl of sugar cubes.

"Shall I charge this to your room?" I ask her.

The woman catches me staring at her black lace dress. "It's vintage. I hope I look like Hedy Lamarr. Or any of the old Hollywood greats. Ava Gardner or Lauren Bacall."

"You already have the air of a starlet." I fake a smile.

"If I could, I'd have von Sternberg direct my life. I want every shot stuffed with curls and golds and exotica. Wouldn't that be fine?" I don't respond. "Does your manager always bother you?"

"Why? Your maternal instincts kicking in?"

"Maternal?" She squints to see if I'm being authentic. "You mean you really couldn't tell?" I shake my head. She's touched by my confusion. "I always worry my throat will be the betrayer." She covers her Adam's apple with her veil. "They tell me my skin is smooth enough to look like Marlene Dietrich's.

Have you seen her films? I own them all, even the crummy westerns. Bought them in Dubai."

"I've only watched the one with her singing in a top hat."

"*Morocco.*"

I start clearing her dishes. I take her cup of cardamom tea. Inside, the dregs make simple shapes. Light bulbs. A marquee. She'll have many fine items to steal, if what she wears is any indication. Her Saturn bracelets, violently gold, brag on their own. And her earring of Chinese blues is far more authentic than the factory pearls most of the debutantes like to parade. I imagine her collection of tiny decadent trinkets I can sell or just toss into the trash with pear-skin scraps. Her florid language, her overly kind eyes. She has the look of someone asking to be jilted. I stare at her necklace of marquise diamonds and seed pearls.

"I had a lover who devastated me among roses," she says. "He gave me these after we skinny-dipped in the pink lake."

"Maharloo?"

She's surprised by my response. "You've been there?"

"I have."

Our long drive. Your CDs of Andy & Kouros, the ones your dad left in the car. In the end, we listened to recordings of Parvin E'tesami's poems set to melancholy violins. The salt water of the pink lake stung my feet because of all my purple blisters. At the time I insisted on wearing dress shoes wherever we went.

As teenagers, we climbed cliffs to undress, a liberating act. To sit on Ravansar nude, we felt no shame. When the wind would start, you'd joke that it was God trying to dress us in sand. We knew it would end, that we'd have to return to the city where we couldn't hold hands for too long.

The air is no longer fresh. Maybe it was before smog carpeted the day, but not now. I walk through the hotel with Leyli under the rows of chandeliers. The hallways on the bottom floor lead to boutiques that are open only by appointment. The salon with draperies covering the latticed windows; the dress shop with Valentino and Gautier gowns, cashmere scarves; a chocolatier that specializes in a bestiary of truffles, leopards and lions and lynxes.

In the indoor garden, the air-conditioning makes belladonnas into bell towers. The rosebushes are still covered with plastic dry-cleaning bags. Each has its own blanket. An employee spray-paints the trees on the periphery white. It's a cheap trick to make them seem alabaster. My uncle touts that the hotel is styled after Persepolis, but it's more of a crass Versailles. The colonnade stinks of orange essence. With all the extravagances, the hallways are still freshened by plug-ins.

"Working here," Leyli says, "I imagine you never want to leave."

"It's true." There are times when I feel I can stay here for weeks without end. And I have done so, when I first escaped from my family and the blood that came as a result of me being caught with a man. But after a while, I got tired of moving from one hotel hallway to the next.

"What floor are you on?" I ask Leyli in the elevator.

"I don't have a room yet. I came to make sure the energy is right in your hotel. I brought this lapis stone a fan sent me from Libya. When you stir it in tea, the water should look blue. That's how you know your spirit is safe. The stone felt warm when I first saw you in the lobby. A good sign. You really think I'm maternal?" She's clearly invested much into my one comment. It's made her feel too comfortable with me. "I almost went to Thailand before I realized they'd pay for half of the surgery if I stayed here." She laughs. "Strange government. Could kill you for being gay, but will foot the bill if you agree to a sex change."

Her words surprise me. She's so direct, it's almost devious.

Leyli sizes up the hotel one more time from the lobby. She nods.

"It's settled. I'll rest here after they cut off my dick."

With that decision, Leyli hurries out into the street. She winds her way through cars with less precision than most. Even teenagers stand back. A truck screeches toward her and barely touches her knee.

"Jackass!" She tightens her veil in her teeth. With both arms free, she pounds the hood. She looks back at me without missing a beat. "You'll help with my going-away party, won't you? Before the last of my surgeries. The big one," she whispers. "God willing. We'll need caviar and zereshk. We'll need archers and stilt-walkers and purebreds. Shall we shop?"

"Right now?"

"Yes. Why, were you busy?"

From her I'm sure I can learn to mimic Marilyn Monroe's walk or Kim Novak's gait. I can steal tricks from Leyli. There are questions about her I prefer to observe rather than ask. Do men stay longer if you have slender wrists? And how a lip curves, does that dictate a different death? As an ingenue to any starlet, I can't startle Leyli with my intentions. Otherwise, I'd be ousted before rehearsing the role of your new wife.

8

Leyli and I step over a rat that was run over by a truck. Red chunks encircle the gray. I can't help but see every dead animal as an omen. A pigeon or a dead dog. They always seem like a threat by someone who wants me gone.

We've finished most of her errands in a day.

"I can't imagine having enough bouquets," Leyli says of her party preparations.

The florist specializes in pastels. The vases are all pink. Past them, my body distorts in glazed ceramics and glass. Those separate selves, are their lives perpendicular to mine or just alternate angles of the same?

"How many bunches?" the florist asks Leyli of the oleander.

She overturns each one to smell them upside down. "As much as you have."

Several bundles are tied with twine and wrapped in a newspaper. Next, a bakery.

"Try one," Leyli says of pink pastries. I haven't had any since my father's death. My mom insisted on baklava, but cried over each piece. I shake my head. She agrees. "Too sweet."

The baker says to Leyli, "They're sweets. They're supposed to be sweet." He leaves to answer the phone in the back.

Leyli doesn't hide her agitation. "You hear how they speak to me? When I'm a full woman, they won't talk to me like that. Even as a young boy, I was bullied. Because I was beautiful, that is why they wanted to make me bleed."

I'm not convinced. "What makes you feel it'll be different?"

"If the agony is even slightly less, I'll be fine. My mother, God rest her soul, she brought me with her to the bakery every Friday. Rice cookies were her treat for our neighbors. She always ordered so quickly, the baker once said, 'Lady, you must know exactly who you are.' I'd like to feel that way, even if for an hour."

In the distance I see a man with a trench coat over his arm. I can feel his breath even from behind the street vendor selling laptop skins. A sigh leaves his mouth and twists around me. He's staring. I want to put my head on the shoulders of a stranger, one who has looked at me for only several minutes, not years of watching me sag with distress.

"You coming?" Leyli asks. To the next destination we go.

The brick house has a tan from vines long cut down. Faint capillaries. Leyli and I walk through a courtyard past potted plants, all dead. She mumbles to herself.

"He didn't water the flowers like he said he would." I figure she's referring to some aggressive lover.

She squashes a deflated soccer ball under her heel. The front gate rattles, a big metallic slab of green. Passing cars, passing cabs. The house is bare. Most things are in boxes. Someone brought in all the fallen branches from a pomegranate tree and placed them in buckets. There is a line of photos around the otherwise empty walls. They start from behind the front door and go all the way around, except for the doorframes leading to other rooms. Each framed photo shows Leyli in her youth. Looks like any little boy in a suit, except Leyli stands in front of crowds on top of stages with opaque lights. In a few backstage shots, the little boy poses with royals and some member of parliament.

"I can't carry it all out myself," Leyli says from above.

I pass empty wall niches on my way up to her. She stands at the top of the stairs and points to an elaborate urn. "I can use that as a gothic ashtray." I try to lift it and nearly knock over the cheap column it rests on.

"Are these yours?"

She nods. "Before the revolution, I was a singer. I was as good as you could be without being an actual castrato. The irony."

Leyli heads into the bedroom where a fully dressed old man sits on a fully made bed. She finds a shoebox under the mattress and empties it of cash. "All this money I sent to make sure you were okay. All the stuff I bought you, old man. But you spent your time kneeled in prayer. I bet you even spend hours praying in your dreams."

Her father doesn't speak. He just turns his head in the opposite direction to pretend she doesn't exist. I can sense the weight of judgment between them. Leyli still talks to him as if there are no hard feelings, even though her father slowly ticks each one of the prayer beads on his strand.

"Can I get you anything?" Leyli asks her father. He doesn't respond. "You have to eat something, old man." He sways back and forth in a room with artichoke flowers painted on the walls. Leyli turns to me. "You mind trying?"

I look in the refrigerator and find only a bottle of blackberry syrup. I stir it with water from the faucet. In the freezer, there are ice cubes shaped like daisies. I pop a few out for him. He takes the glass from me and sets it down on the carpet next to his feet.

Leyli shrugs after we leave.

"I may look like a woman who has it all together, but it's taxing."

I can't ask her all my questions. I want to, but can't. She'd call me a fraud. I don't mind being a man, not really. But a man with the stubborn desire for other men, that was always a vein I wanted to peel from my wrist.

"I can go grab your father something to eat."

"He's just being dramatic. Ever since he stopped talking to me, he's fatter than he's ever been."

The butcher laughs when I tell him the slaughterhouse smells like sugar.

"My wife uses caramel to wax our neighbors. Sometimes you can't tell the difference between animals and the women getting plucked." He cackles in such a cruel way, as if slitting the neck of a calf is nothing more than scissoring the hem of a sleeve. "We have a live lamb out back. You want it?"

Leyli thinks it over. "Red meat bores me, but my guests might like it." She turns to me. "What do you think?"

The butcher hurries her away before I can give my opinion. "Come, watch me cut off its head."

Leyli leaves behind her purse. I can snag a few bills, that's all. Just a few to get my escape started. But the smell of her rose perfume stops me.

I wait outside the butcher shop and tag behind a faucet hose with graffiti pens. Nothing drastic. I color in the shadow at this particular time of day. I share a sordid intimacy with a man outside who doesn't realize I can see him taking a piss. He doesn't aim at the corner, but puts his back on the wall and pisses with the wind. In the distance the lamb is severed from its neck. The sound is unmistakable, no matter what the butcher says. The poor dead beast. It reminds me of the alchemies from *The Book of the Cow*, the spells involving a female calf cut from its head and sewn at its orifices. I read about it in my mother's note cards on Al-Simawi and alchemy. She underlined how to make a house appear full of snakes.

Outside the butcher, I hear the shuffle, a wail. I picture it in a strobe. You and the other man. His hand on your hip. You kiss him and he kisses back. A kick, a kick, another kick.

I never told you about the time I went to visit my grandma and found her covering her roses with burlap sacks that once held basmati rice.

"To keep the deer from eating them," she swore.

I helped as much as I could when she covered them, and hours later I helped take the sacks off. I paused at one rosebush when I saw a glimmer. Left behind from the basmati label was the tiniest thread of gold wrapped around one of the thorns. That moment reverberates whenever I see a man shake the final ribbons of piss or cum from his dick. Now, for a moment I feel closer to this stranger on the street than I do to you.

Leyli returns in a light sweat.

"He'll deliver the body later. For the party, I'll cook the face." She has it wrapped up. I refuse to hold the head on the cab ride to the hotel. "Just for one moment."

She plops it onto my crotch. She opens her purse to get out the cab fare. It reminds me of you, your weight in my lap.

"Right here is fine," Leyli tells the cab driver. I return the lamb's head to her. On my thigh, a drop of its juice. "No need to cringe. You look so sickly. I mainly got it for you."

I apologize to the head, as would any unintentional Salome. But I am not afraid. I grew up with death. It was the third person in my parents' marriage. It was the ongoing conversation my mother had, all the times she tried to hang herself with plastic rope because of a sorrow she couldn't put into words.

"You are your mother's son," you'd say, knowing that hurt me most.

I picture myself hanging from a citron tree, birds gathering around me until I exhale the last ounce of sweetness from my chest.

9

The city is awake today. Other days it might droop. But today, the people stand upright because they know I will see you soon. I swing my plastic bag of condoms and apricots. They match by coincidence, based on the quickest stock the salesman wrangled from under his counter while his wife adjusted the saffron display. In my right hand, I hold the quart of cream. I've learned from experience that if I leave the carton in the grocery bag, it'll soak everything in whiteness. The market is three blocks from the apartment and nine blocks from the hotel.

Someone pushes me from behind. I drop the carton of cream. It splashes upward. I look down at it instead of up, away in anticipation of what I expect to take place. A knife to my throat. The prelude to a beating. My mind always turns to violence.

I hope to see you when I look up.

"Hello, stranger," you'd say. Your greeting.

"Strange hello." My response. "You're back."

"I had to see you." A rarity. "No, not a rarity." You'd hear my thoughts.

You'd push me into an alley sick with expired yogurt, mop filth, and a carton of fresh cream. But our kiss would change it all. Gnats would turn to moths. I always swore they were sweeter than butterflies, maybe because you told me they were powdered with sugar.

You'd pull my hair so it hit the brick wall, one with grout that stamps an empty graph onto my back. I'd taste blood in our kisses because you always bite my bottom lip too deeply.

I blink and the moment dissolves. You didn't knock me down. It was just some kid chasing his rubber ball. I remember my next errand.

I still need the samovar repaired before you return from the hospital. The one I broke really is the best at telling fortunes. From its kettle, tea dregs would reach upward in reverse ripples, dying to be read by me. Other samovars are amateurs. I see nothing in their stains. After our last fight, I knocked it over. Now I want it back.

The man at the orchid bazaar selling remote controls to outdated Sony sets, I can tell he's well-endowed by the way he sits. He's too polite to reposition himself. I'd try my damnedest to help him untangle. I should have more goals, shouldn't I? Grander than cum, and deeper than what'll fit.

"Get your thumb out your ass," my uncle would say when back in town. Did he know what I did with my ring finger, betrothed to myself? It was one of the many things we argued about.

"Can you fix it?" I ask the man at the orchid bazaar. He turns the samovar around. His three sons watch a soccer game on TV. When they near the screen, the set goes black.

The man sets down the samovar. "Why don't I show you a new model, one that turns off by itself?" He looks at the broken picture frame in my hand. He sizes up the cracked glass severing our lips. "That your brother?"

"Of course." Telling people we're relatives, not lovers, encompasses our history more accurately.

The colors in the picture haven't faded. We stand in front of the Tomb of Hafiz, the only place I insisted on a photo of us together. I whirled to make the octagonal dome circular in my dizziness. You backed into the columns with polygons at the top and snapped a photo of me when I collapsed. We ran past the demons in the cypresses, the pearls in the gooseberry shrubs until the high ended. In the photo of us together, we lean on ruined pillars from a rainstorm that should have been named.

The repairman yells for his wife. She enters peeling a radish. She looks at the samovar and the broken glass of the picture frame. "Was it a quarrel?"

"A break-in."

"And they went after this old thing?" She shakes her head. "We have newer models too, some with fancy high-tech screens. You can bring the water to a boil or a slight simmer. A samovar with a digital face, wouldn't that be nice?"

"No, thanks."

"Not even a samovar with a heat-resistant handle?"

"I'm fine with a few burns."

She laughs. She tosses a clean radish into a bowl. "You must be real sentimental."

"It belonged to someone I loved."

"A keepsake?"

I nod. I am the boy with the Midas tongue. I make keepsakes of men.

10

A new waiting game at the hospital before you're fit to leave. I put cherries on the bridge of my nose while leaning back. Each one that rolls left means yes. Each one that rolls right, no. Will we ever leave together? Three right. Three left. The last one, left too. Yes.

On a whim I invent alternate versions of us. In Paris we eat cheeseburgers with too much salt. You tell me you've slept with someone else. We laugh about it, but I don't share my mille-feuille. Would I still love you there? Three cherries, yes. Four cherries, no.

In Senegal. We drink bissap juice in a high-rise. During sunset we peel spirals from pear skins. Who can make the longest snake? You tell me you've slept with someone else. Would I still love you there? Two cherries, yes. Four cherries, no.

In Tangier. No, no, and no. I'd leave you there and love would leave from me.

Two nurses wheel you out to the curb.

"Ready to go home?" they ask.

You are finally mine to take. I don't know how to be a caregiver. Do I pat the top of your head? I should have rehearsed being gentler, but it would hardly stick, like a terrible actor who drops his accent midway through a performance.

We reach my uncle's apartment. Will you react to the roses? For ceremony, I took the vases out of the closet and set them under the lamps with the largest bulbs. I've arranged them as a minor distraction from what I can't bring myself to change. In the living room, two cups. On the floor, a sock, a shoe.

I expect a far more dramatic scene when you enter our apartment, as if you'll size up what you'd left behind, the glasses, and all the dander in its place. But you are expressionless. You inhale deeply, like one does before passing a dumpster, and you excuse yourself into the room safe from the memory. We don't bring up the conversation that made you run away.

I lock the front door. Alone, we kiss. Your lips are swollen. As a welcome, I end up on my knees. At your feet, always. It's where I am most like myself. You feel too dirty to even shower yet. There's only so much cleaning that can take place in a hospital with a sponge. But I don't care. I dive into the stench of pooled crotch sweat in unwashed seams. Gray jeans, once black. While blowing you, I think about your clothes. They were cruel to make you squeeze back into your old pants from the night of the attack. If I'd noticed, I would have brought you a different pair.

Once your dick is in my mouth, it becomes commonplace. I'm curious to see how much you can take despite all your lacerations. My pleasure is inseparable from your pain. I make a few noises to prove I'm still present. Your eyes roll back, maybe because you want me to stop. I try not to sneeze when your pubes tickle my nostrils. Part of me hopes to taste the other young man. Your pleasure is inseparable from my pain.

"The old war. The old war." A man mumbles to himself on his way through our alley.

You inch toward the bed, struggling to remove the hospital gown that also acts as your shirt. You reach for a painkiller after I wipe my chin clean. I look up at the skylight in the living room. At this hour I hope to see a face above the glass, someone who has found his way to the top of the seventh floor of the Sohlem Apartments, which we like to call Sodom. No faces above. Sometimes a few rats scurry past. They are the only witnesses to our version of paradise.

"Did you eat?" I ask.

You shake your head.

I'm not used to being the one in power, but pain has made you malleable. I can whisper thoughts so they catch deep enough in you. When you are upright again, when you have your hands around my neck, you might say my words like they're yours.

Let's leave. Far enough, but not too far.

"Humiliate me," you say from the corner of the bed. I'm not sure what you mean. I dab the dotted ring of dried blood around your lips. Death used to be distant. A dead crow, a body lowered into a grave. Not now. Outside, a truck sells honeydew for those still awake.

"Ripe and cheap."

The vendor repeats it three times on a megaphone. Ripe and cheap.

You pucker your mouth to try and apologize. I kiss you to shut you up. I lick your lips. Bruised, they sting. I press your velvet gums with my tongue. I rub them one way, smooth. The other way, your chin fills with blood. You moan. You try to apologize.

"You shouldn't speak until your teeth have set."

I wonder what your voice will sound like over that chasm. Maybe they kicked your vocal cords and shook the box. Did a man find a tooth stuck to his shoe after you were down?

I squeeze an orange to your mouth. You used to boil them to remove the bitterness from their skin. On a dare, you drank the liquid they left behind, all pith, just to impress me. Maybe with these memories, you will agree to my plan. The juice spills down your throat. A spurt, a cut-open vein. You moan. Pain—it comes back.

I pull out the box of bootleg VHS tapes and search for a quieter film to fill the silence.

You repeat yourself. "Humiliate me. So we're even."

"I don't need to."

"Please. Humiliate me. Before we move on to what comes next."

What comes next?

"The old war."

The same man paces up and down our street. We're sure he has no home. Every morning he sells walnuts in emptied pita bread bags. He cracks the walnuts at night, puts on his army beret in the morning, and walks down the streets trying to sell what he can. His hands are black with walnut skins. His lips are dry from a diet of almonds in brine.

I invite him up.

He tries to find something to say. "The old war." I undo his jacket once he's inside. "The old war."

You breathe out of your nose now, some recent habit after having your jaw wired to heal. It makes it easier to gauge your mood. You breathe heavier when I'm close to him. I hold my cheek to his neck. Mouth open, you finally show your new teeth.

"Is this okay?" I ask the man.

He nods. I take off his coat and place it on the couch. Even if he's here for my own selfish game, I treat him kindly. The slightest kiss will be something he'll replay with himself while cracking walnuts, which I smell in his mouth, curdled, without the aid of a toothbrush to clean off the plaque. But you stay in the shadows just to watch me put his hand on his own dick to see if I can make him cream at our feet.

Accidentally, you scratch an itch you've forgotten was there.

"God!" The pain makes you double over.

I turn to the walnut vendor. "Take anything you want in the kitchen." He follows the sound of the refrigerator out of the room. "Are you all right?" I ask when I'm by your side. "What can I do?"

You hear the crack in my voice. I could joke that my throat is hoarse because your cum is infecting my tonsils again. But

I don't make light. This startles you even more than pain. We know the truth. If there was one more kick, if someone aimed their foot a little higher up, you'd be dead.

"Mahtob is my wife," you whisper. I recognize your tone. Aggressive, yes, but also exhausted from running through the different scenarios. "Isn't running to Isfahan enough?"

"I used to think so. But there needs to be a change."

"What change?"

"We'll be safe . . . once you remarry." After a pause, you get what I mean. We'll be safe when I'm your bride.

"I can't ask that of you," you say. The painkillers start the dance of making you drowsy.

"I have to. I'll do it all."

"But—"

"There are no other options. I just need you to agree."

I head out of the room to give you time to think.

"Can I get you something to eat?" I ask our guest in the kitchen. He's entranced by the clean water I keep in a pitcher.

He gestures at it. "May I?"

"Of course."

I look for a glass, but he's already chosen a tulip-shaped crystal vase, freshly washed for your return. He fills it with as much water as it can take. Blueness takes hold of the living room. You've turned on the TV. I stand on the threshold of the kitchen and the living room to see what film you've chosen.

The Postman Always Rings Twice, poorly dubbed in Persian. It was the only version you could find. The translation might not be faithful, but I get the gist. Lana Turner and John Garfield embrace each other while plotting to kill her husband.

"What if we get caught?" his dubbed voice asks her.

"We won't. Not if we're smart about it."

The tape warps for a minute, some transfer error from torrent to tape. A large wave contorts their faces.

"This must be love," he says.

"It's got to be," she responds. "Otherwise it wouldn't be worth it."

With that, I know you're on board. You've chosen the scene as proof. Your eyes roll back already on the way to sleep. I'll never forget the violence at their edge.

11

When I arrive at her party, Leyli doesn't fake propriety. She kisses me on both cheeks like we know each other well. Even your aunt started to give me handshakes once I reached puberty. Leyli, however, treats me like we're old friends.

"Does this look wrinkled?" she asks of some sequin monstrosity. "I never iron my dresses. I only caress them. It was either this or some Shanghai Lily concoction. See the Weimar influence?"

Three hotel maids help her prepare for the evening. The first attendant polishes swan embellishments for her hair. She fluffs, curls, and straightens the wigs, so Leyli has her pick for the night. The second maid lights the candles around the room. Most of them are taken out of boxes and given a sheen with a lace rag. A third maid cleans all the mirrors in the place. She polishes the candelabras with ornate Albanian bases.

"You like Italian?" Leyli asks. "I know a half-Italian I think you'll love."

"No, thanks."

"He won't bite."

"He?"

"Oh, we're being coy." She lies down on the ground to brush her sable cape all in one direction. The fur points eastward. Leyli swings her fur coat over her chest to inspect the collar.

It isn't clear which of her guests arrives first. After inspecting the books on her shelves, most of them Wilde, I turn around to multiple foursomes undoing their coats. One of her friends arrives with a cardigan over her shoulders.

She looks me over. "Is he safe?"

"Of course," Leyli replies. "Can't you tell? He wears his heartbreak on his sleeve."

The guest tears off her veil. I already feel overdressed in my formal work attire: black slacks, white gloves, my dress shirt and tie. I watch as Leyli kisses her guests once on each cheek. She holds her face to theirs and lets the only contact be from cheekbone to cheekbone while feigning a kiss through its sound.

"Oh, God," one of her guests says after giving me a once-over. She sneers in my direction. "How clever to invite a mime." They laugh. I remove my gloves and place them in my back pocket. I play off my embarrassment.

A man arrives with a centerpiece of roses and dahlias and lotus threads, all red. He says, "To hang over you while you're recovering in bed."

Leyli smiles. "I'll be in bed, but I won't recover. I'll be ravaged."

Among her friends, I can't tell if Leyli is becoming less or more of herself. I expected stability in her image, but that was my mistake. She is no starlet. A prop master, maybe, one who knows how to stuff the scene to hide the absences.

Leyli puts her arm around me. "Now, dear. Wouldn't it make more sense if you kept on your gloves?" It hits me. I'm not here as a guest. All the more reason to deceive them all. Leyli motions to a crate of wine bottles. "You won't tell on me, will you? I can't afford to pay someone else off."

I uncork the bottles of smuggled Shiraz. A few women are wearing expensive earrings underneath their scarves. The thin satin on their heads does nothing to hide their jewelry. After a couple of swigs of wine, their hijabs come off too.

One of them leaps up. "I feel absolutely electric! Wasn't it Tennyson who warned of a snake turning into a dragon?"

I interrupt. "It was Rumi."

She rolls her eyes. "I should know. I've been a Libra for at least three millennia." The woman in a leopard shawl embraces Leyli from behind. "Darling, with you as a woman, how can I compete?"

"Simple. Become a man."

"I'd go mad with a dick." They each try to outlaugh the other. It goes on for three beats too long.

"You're too lucid," Leyli says when I head into the kitchen. "No need to take it personally. I just needed a little extra help." She grabs a shot of whiskey for me and sets it down next to an orange chaise. "Sit." I sit. Under my glass, a playing card is a coaster. A suicide king.

"What are the chances?" The man next to me holds up his coaster, his card. Another of the same. "I wonder what that means, two suicide kings."

"A fallen dynasty."

Leyli whispers in my ear from behind the chair. "Did you notice his accent?" I shake my head. "Half-Italian."

For some awful reason, he wants to get to know me.

"We've met before," he says.

"Unlikely."

"Probably in Al-Andalus Garden." He's trying to prove he's well traveled, as if it would impress me. "My favorite place in Cairo."

"How do you know Leyli?"

"See that guy?" He points to one in a bowler hat. "He invited me. I'm in the suite on the seventh floor."

"The bachelor units?"

"Just for a few months. Close enough to Laleh Park and the museum. Only while the internship lasts."

"Where?"

"The Tehran Museum of Contemporary Art. You been?"

"Perhaps."

Omid opens his mouth all the way when he smiles. It's the only thing that makes his large eyes shrink behind his glasses. He has no harsh edges on his face. His chin, his nose both look sanded smooth. This gentleness probably carries into the bedroom where he has peaceful, quiet sex.

"Anjir." He repeats my name. I wonder how he looks when he creams.

I hear your voice. *Humiliate me. So we're even.*

It would provide symmetry. Stability until we can execute our plan.

I lean close to Omid. "I was named after the fig tree my mom had in her yard. Anjirs are her favorite fruit. The comedy of it all. No fig has been pumped with more seed than me."

Leyli interrupts by grabbing my arm. "Baby doll, can you stock up on ice?"

I call the concierge. After several minutes, Panj wheels in a service cart with five buckets of ice. The corner of each bucket has a stain from price-tag adhesives that couldn't be cleaned off completely. Leyli looks over the stock of ice in disgust.

"Is this not enough?" Panj asks.

"No, honey. Not real ice. Cocaine." Her friends laugh.

Panj smiles, a rarity around strangers. There's a difference in her demeanor. I realize why. Her gray tooth has been replaced with a shiny new white fake. Now instead of standing out from the rest for being too dark, it's the brightest single tooth in the room.

"Simple mistake." A party guest in elbow-length gloves says to Panj before slapping her ass.

"Could have fooled me," another jokes. "She looks like she's snorted it all."

"Leave her alone," I say.

For interrupting, I become the focal point of the cult.

"I didn't know we had a prude among us," one of them says. "How chivalrous."

"Do you know any particular tricks or parlor games?" another asks.

The woman in the leopard shawl laughs. "Of course he does. He probably scrubs toilets well."

Panj speaks up for me. "He reads tea leaves."

"You've been holding out on us. Why not prove it?"

I hate the attention, but anything to shut them up.

From the closet, two maids pull out a samovar. They plug it in and bring water in a crystal bowl emptied of its spiked punch. It takes three trips to the faucet to fill the samovar. A man in a tuxedo clears a seat next to Leyli.

She inches closer to me and says, "Wouldn't it be more appropriate without those gloves?"

I take them off and head for the door.

"Leaving already?" someone yells.

"I'll have to bring some special tea."

Our corner room on the twelfth floor of the hotel has what I need. Many drugs hide behind the velvet Venus in the velvet safe in our room. I check my chess set with inlay mosaics of pewter and mother-of-pearl. In the drawer, under each chess piece, I keep options to fuck off for a day. It's taken years to stockpile enough acid for the queen. Ketamine for the king. Hash for the rook. The bishop prefers miscellany to turn any drink gold or any drink blue. I collect sticky pearls for every hothouse tongue.

Leyli and her friends deserve something cheap, mandrakes that'll make them pass out and give them all gurgly shits. Back at the party, I oversteep the Earl Grey on purpose so they don't taste a thing. Panj helps pass out cups to every guest.

"How will we know when it's ready to drink?" someone asks.

Panj helps me with the act. "To kill time, everyone think of a first to share."

"A first what?"

"A first anything. By the time you choose one, your drink will be ready to sip."

During the silence at Leyli's party, I turn over my tea. I see all that I've lost, but I won't admit it. A smile for the close-up, a wrinkle for the cut. What would I choose? I wouldn't know what to say about our first fuck, because sex with us happened slowly over years. You walked in on me jacking off, and you stayed. I did the same with you. We just sat there, eventually putting our heads closer to each other's laps, not to swallow, but to keep each other company with our heat. From my crotch to your face, from your dick to my cheeks. And then you put it on my lips, but only for a few strokes. And then you finished off on my ear. To say it was once, or one encounter, or one day is a fallacy. We for months were fumbling toward sex.

"What do you want to know?" Panj asks Leyli after she's finished her tea. "Past, present, or future?" Panj has chosen the role of my assistant.

"It doesn't matter. So long as he proves himself."

A worthy challenge.

"Hand it over," says a man with a cigarette behind his ear. Down the line Leyli's guests pass her teacup, still upside down on a saucer so the dregs can bleed shapes.

"Gently!" Panj says when one almost drops the glass.

Truly it makes no difference. Even obscured, even if the symbols pivot or blur, what's left would still give insight.

"Go on. What do you see?" Leyli hovers off the edge of her chaise.

She wants it so badly, some fluff about her choices being aligned with her destiny. I can give her the gift of an intimate deceit. I don't need to turn the glass much to give my first impression as a reading.

"A braid."

I swear someone gasps.

"A braid?!"

"That hardly seems right!"

I continue: "A big, fat braid."

"Are you sure it's not a gorgon?" a cattier friend jokes.

"I should hope not," Leyli says. "Though I've been called worse."

Her friends laugh. "A braid? She'd never!"

"Not with her flare for glamour."

But we make eye contact, Leyli and me, an arrow through the drunken caws. A wig with a simple braid. Something she hasn't told anybody. For her, ordinariness is a respite she'd sometimes prefer. We meet somewhere in between our desires to be unbothered. Her as a woman, me as a lover, not with our eyes toward perfection. Our lives will never be so. But to minimize agony when possible.

After a pause, the man with a cigarette behind his ear interrupts.

"Yes. I see it too." He grabs the cup from me. "A braid."

"Where?" the woman next to him asks.

"Hidden right there."

"A braid!"

A tickle waves through the guests. Their collective laughter starts closest to the door and spreads across the room, before becoming a yawn that ricochets the other way. Now good and drunk, Leyli's guests open an entryway closet to rummage through her expensive, human-hair wigs. Not like the synthetics my grandmother wore after chemo. She put on her cheap hair before leaving the house, even though her veil covered it all. Three of Leyli's guests start trying on different hairstyles. They're too drunk to notice me sizing up their jewels.

"This one's a bitch," a guest says of Louise Brooks's bob.

"A flapper," Leyli corrects her.

Another drunk guest tries on a sinuous nightmare of a wig.

"Some of these are hardly practical." She points to the locks coiled around wires to look like tentacles. "Don't tell me it's another Dietrich."

"Close," Leyli says with her eyes barely open. "Another of Josef von Sternberg's beasts. But I'd have to say my favorite femme fatale is Greta Garbo as Mata Hari, even though no one would believe Ramon Novarro as her love interest. That fag couldn't woo a pile of burning sticks." She makes herself laugh. She's too drugged to be discreet. "This would make quite a prompt for the interview. *Which movie starlet is your favorite and why?*"

"What interview?" a friend asks.

"To get the country to approve the surgery."

I slither around the party to take what I want from necks and throats and wrists. I snatch an earring of spinel stones from someone sitting on the couch, and a yellow-diamond thumb ring from someone in the kitchenette. The trick is to steal little enough so they won't notice until well into tomorrow, or won't have the nerve to mention for fear of sounding trite. I can't overlook Leyli's wealth. She and her guests afford a reality that suits them. For me, it's work. For me, it's scrounging. My father would say these socialites come from families who stole their wealth during the revolution.

As other wigs are tossed on and off, Grace Kelly locks and Veronica Lake bangs, I continue my mission. Removing some jewels is important, not to steal but to scatter around the room to give the idea that in their stupor, these socialites just hurled their inscribed rose combs from the balcony, did the same with iron-red cuff links, or tossed in their amethyst wristwatches for a poker game. I hand Panj a bracelet of mandarin garnets.

In Leyli's bedroom, a mannequin head with live poppies in its mouth sits on her dresser. Her most precious treasure not only glows but levitates a few inches to be seen: a necklace of seed pearls and marquise diamonds. It's ridiculous on me. In her mirror, there isn't a moment of rightness where I feel like I'm finally where I am meant to be. Instead, I just see myself wearing pearls, plain and ordinary.

Her mirror has toothpaste splattered in the right corner. Spittle on the glass aligns with my lips. Appropriately, I'm rabid for revenge. It's esoteric rage, not directed clearly at anyone, not at the men who assaulted you, or the cypress trees that did not intervene during the attack. It's different to indulge in our own violence of broken glassware and spit up cherries from an argument during a meal. Fear of your death, the worry of being slaughtered. That is why I'm here. One brutality too many brought me to this mirror, surrounded by Leyli's leftover exhales from powdering herself smooth as part of her regimen.

Under her bed, I find something far more valuable. She has shoeboxes full of estrogen pills, as if she's stocked up for years. The prescription is in Persian, with the name of a pharmacy I recognize. She won't have difficulty getting more.

Would it be easier if I underwent the change? I know the answer. It's not about making life easier. It's a matter of staying alive to have more time with you, to be able to pick each other's stray eyelashes safely without worrying about execution.

Becoming and unbecoming is no leap. I take two of Leyli's pills, and with them, I accept the mission. I keep our love a secret like travelers to Mecca long ago would swallow their treasures to keep them safe from robbers during their pilgrimage. Eventually thieves started gutting pilgrims to dig for gold in their intestines. Our life of secrecy isn't safe anymore.

I snag the pearls off Leyli's mannequin head and lower the strand into my pocket. It makes a second bulge. Several of her prescription bottles fit perfectly in my sleeves. I take her estrogen pills with me. Enough, but not too much.

I turn around when I hear him laugh. Omid, the half-Italian.

"I'll keep your secret if you keep me company."

He puts a whiskey bottle on the bedside table. A dare. I down half.

12

The moon is an awkward pink. As a kid I thought there were different moons. The full, the crescent. Waxing and waning. I gave each shape a name.

Omid smiles. "Leyli's quite the matchmaker."

They make me sick, his even, tablecloth teeth. With Omid, the way he looks at me, I can tell. Perhaps it's the depth of my grief, it heightens other talents: restlessness, falling into orifices. Omid wants to hold my hand. He wants to brush my hair back. A kiss, perhaps. But the punch line: it will always end with brutality. A bullet that pulls the string off our teeth, or even the acid death of aging. It'd be too easy to kiss him. Like a Caravaggio still life, I need it to take place shrouded in darkness, with the shit smells of a latrine, or near a stone tower built by two boys.

Omid and I walk to Haft-Hoze. Some people eat faloodeh. Kids fight over who can eat the most limes. Teens kick a soccer ball with a police guard. A kick, a kick, a kick.

"I bet it's difficult to have relationships here."

He's right. I've never had to admit it to a stranger before, but I also don't want his pity.

"You have anyone waiting for you back home?"

"Kinda." He loosens up when he realizes I'll never meet anyone from his life in Taranto. He chugs a disgusting gulp from his flask and hands it to me.

"You sleep with women too?" I ask.

"Just once. I didn't enjoy it." He tries to recover from his candor. "It probably won't be the last." He can tell I'm distracted. "You thinking about someone else?"

"Yup."

"You love him?"

"We had plans."

"For your future?"

"For our past."

I go quiet once we reach our destination. Omid stays outside and stares into a store window with antique pocket watches on display. I stop at the blackboard at the entrance of a boutique, where the owner usually writes inspirational sayings. The day's quote has already been wiped clean, but I see Hafiz's name jotted at the bottom. The jeweler finishes his night prayer. Around him, all the plush trays are empty, save for a few safflowers spaced out for color reference.

"Still here?" I ask.

"There's always something to polish." The jeweler peels a nectarine while I dump out my finds. Emeralds enticing enough to eat. Cloudless carmine. A crucible of rubies. He gasps. "It's as if you've scattered the sky on my lap." He points to the necklace of Leyli's marquise diamonds. "That too?" I could. It'd be easy to get rid of her precious stock.

"Nah. I'll keep this one for myself."

He inspects the jewels in front of him. After a moment, he pushes them back.

"I won them," I say to ward off his suspicions.

He knows me too well. "I still can't. Not in good conscience."

"Mull it over."

"Truthfully, you can only do so much with these treasures. They're too hot. Let's say they get reported. It would be easy to trace them back to me and I would give up your name without hesitation if there's any threat." He pushes his appraisal tray back to me. "No one will feel comfortable trying to sell. Not for a month or three."

"It isn't for the money," I lie. "Just the thrill."

"Dear boy, there must be gentler thrills." He can tell I'm dejected. "Have you tried the bazaar? By the rug district. They'll buy or sell any number of things."

"Sure, sure."

"The moon has changed," Omid says when we reunite outside.

I look up. No longer pink. Omid elbows my side and continues talking before I have a chance to respond. "Maybe we should go back to your place." He's plastered. I'm drunk too.

Our taxi speeds down the freeway past Day-Glo graffiti of martyrs I can't name. Omid pulls a slab of my hair. "I'd like to draw you."

I hope you're awake to see me enter with him. I hope you're awake to humiliate. In my drunken haze, it makes a wild amount of sense to me: to cleanse the palate. And afterward, we can coordinate the last of our plans.

Omid looks at his hand and thinks about what he can do with each of his fingers. Wrap them around any part of my body. Neck, dick, ankles.

"I think we're being followed." He's too drunk to take seriously.

"Sure."

"Really. Check."

A car behind our cab. Is it familiar?

I whisper in Omid's ear. "Everyone should have someone who wants them dead. It means you're doing something right."

He stops shifting and puts his hand on my lap. Upstairs, our curtains. Do they move? Or are you already in bed? You'll pleasure yourself until nameless and blind. I'll go with Omid to Taranto. It'll be me and him now. Maybe you were right, and we share too much history. We were each other's first everything. How cruel to find love on the first try.

"Kiss me," Omid says in the elevator.

"In a minute."

I'm disappointed you're not on the couch when he enters the apartment. Omid picks up my children's book of Greek mythology next to the TV and nervously taps his fingers on the cover like it's a tombak.

"You play other percussion instruments?" I ask while I try to regain some sobriety.

He's surprised I've noticed.

"No. Not yet."

He's all talk. Omid doesn't know how to initiate. Drunkenness gets him partway, but he still has no tact. The way he moves, I can tell he has to piss before trying to get it up.

"I'm sorry, I'm sorry." You call out from the bedroom. We both turn.

"Who's that?" Omid asks. He wasn't anticipating an audience. He panics like any man plotting his escape.

"A spectator."

"I'm sorry, I'm sorry." We hear you from the bedroom again.

Omid shakes his head. "I . . . I can't."

He thinks he's slick with his escape, but I can tell he'd even crack the doors off their hinges to leave. It's his own deception that makes him pull the door when he knows it needs to be pushed. Embarrassed, he hurries down the stairs. The trap sets him free.

When alone, I go into the bedroom. I feel eyes prying, peeking out of windows and from the center of pansies just to watch me. You're not there. The balcony door is open.

Below I expect to see a splatter with your silhouette. But no. The walnut vendor sits on the street next to a fountain with coins no one will touch.

"I'm sorry, I'm sorry." He yells a new sentence. Near him, a black cat looks at me. Its eyes catch light from a source I can't see. Its tail pricks up, fur on only half. The taunt is subtle. I turn away. On our bed, you've left a note.

13

Four words only. An unfair note.
The miracle. Book 3.

A cruel riddle, especially when I'm so whiskey drunk. You are gone. It's clear. Despite your frailty, you've found a way to leave. Your clothes are missing, the bare hangers spread between my pants and shirts with too few buttons.

The kitchen trash can is empty. You've even set a new bag. I check the living room closet. The giant box that held our monstrous samovar is missing too. You must have used it to carry your scant belongings.

An ejected tape is still in the VCR. *The Postman Always Rings Twice.* I pop it back in and press play. The film is gone. Recorded over with nothingness.

Book three. I can't quite figure out what you mean. On the shelf, I count three from each side, but get motion sick from too much movement. I tear through what I can to find a reference. None in book three of Rumi's *Masnavi.* And the third cantos of heaven, hell, and purgatory tell me nothing. Neither does *Pantagruel.* If you had ripped the page out of the book directly, it'd have been easier. But perhaps you didn't want to leave evidence. I look for notes hidden behind the hallway sconces. I don't find any.

Did you mean Al-Dimiri, who wrote that dreams of snakes predict wealth? Is it a Brothers Grimm reference? Are you hoping I'll take a bite of a white snake in order to speak to animals? Perhaps it's a joke about oral sex, or one about how you're ready to leave me.

I should know. I'm rarely stumped by your references. I pride myself on being well-read. When I fed you bulgur soup during your last bout of migraines, you said: "Who are you, Nizami's snake?" That was an easier one. In the Persian epic romance, Majnun keeps watch like a serpent over his dead lover's grave.

Moths circle around me when I open the window. They charge the corners of the room, not the light bulbs. They get clobbered in the books I open and shut looking for a reference to miracles and snakes and roses and pearls, a vague enough note that could keep me looking forever.

Moths get smashed in books of Goya illustrations, notes in a Marguerite Duras memoir, also in *The Blind Owl*. Gnats die in the pages of a Persian-English dictionary, somewhere close to where the book switches languages, and the pages are flipped upside down for the English portion. We can still escape to Isfahan, where we first fucked, to the hotel where we take our yearly trip. It's dangerous trying to build a life in a memory, I know.

You're cruel to leave me with a riddle you thought I might get on the first try. I pull out the dresser drawers in the bedroom to hide Leyli's jewels before I pass out (I know I will). I need her diamonds and stones hidden from view until I can try to sell them again.

My crotch rubs against the dresser when I put away the loot, and I realize you might never see my hard-on again. It's enough to get me stiff, to want to rub your boxers into my nostrils. But you've taken them all with you. There is one pair of my boxers you borrowed on some night when you stayed even though you hadn't planned to. Seeing you in my underwear turned me on, watching your morning wood slip through my flap.

I try to get myself off, but instead I feel a gurgle come up my throat, thicker than a belch, a chunk of the day. It's only liquid, some small bubbling amount I throw up. I've been so focused on feeding you orange slices and escape strategies, I've hardly eaten.

What a waste, I think after heaving. I must have thrown up some of Leyli's pills. One dose less. I crawl back to the bedroom. A vigil of birds lands on the balcony. The dresser drawers sit next to me on the floor. I stick my head deep in the cavity of the bureau for some safe darkness. Not unlike a limp body in a lukewarm tub, I fall under.

14

I wake up to catch the tail end of a message on the landline. It's the next day, though from where I'm lying on the bedroom floor, yesterday and today feel the same.

Thankfully I had enough tact to pull my head out of the dresser emptied of its drawers. I shoved my boxers behind my neck for a pillow, though the wood floors left pinstripe indentations on my back. I must have kicked off most of my clothes pretending you were blowing me before giving up.

I check the answering machine.

"You woke me up from my dream," Leyli says on the message. "Just as I was telling Alain Delon where he could put it, your face popped into my head." She suspects I've stolen from her and her friends. I know it. Sounds like she's chewing wet chocolate cherries. "I wanted to make sure Omid was a gentleman. Unless he's still there? I hope I didn't scare you off with one of my garish parties. My friends are assholes. I barely confide in any of them."

Turns out the guilt is her own. She's trying to relate to me. I'm her version of slumming.

Under the couch, I see a tiny glimmer of plastic. At some point, the hospital bag must have gotten knocked behind the couch and lodged against the wall. I'm surprised you didn't take it with you, like you did all other mementos. Including the used condom, just the one, even though you two could have fucked multiple times without any latex between you.

After a long pause, Leyli finishes her message. "You're lucky. You've found someone to be with. I thought you'd be my protégé, but maybe it's the other way around." She hangs up.

From the plastic hospital bag, I finally pull out your shirt. I can't unfold it. It's too stiff and purple with blood from the night you were attacked. The moths know to keep away. I lay the bloody shirt on the couch cushions. There are no clues on the collar. No writing, just a ring of blue. How cleanly the rest was dyed by your blood.

Three soft knocks accompany the thought. Someone is at the door. I throw it open expecting it to be you, to help solve the riddle or to call the whole thing off. Once the door is flung open, once I'm met by the starkness of eyes the same color as mine, I realize I'm no closer to understanding your note. I have no time to practice a reaction.

"Oh."

All I can think to say. Better not to say more, even though I haven't seen him since he tried to end my life.

"Oh." My brother says the same thing right back.

He's surprised to see me in the apartment, but covers it up by swatting at a moth. It's my fault for leaving the balcony door open all night. Now the walls have uneven dots that gather around a framed photo of a Matisse. My brother and I avoid eye contact. Was he expecting to see you here?

Clearly he hasn't slept in weeks, except for the length of a sigh. I can't lie and tell him he looks good when his skin is so gray and his teeth are eating themselves from outside in. As teens, we might have smoked a few joints together, ones I found when I started working at the hotel. I didn't bring him any stronger drugs, even though I still wonder about my role in his addiction.

My brother covers his face for a sneeze that never comes. From his pocket a credit card falls out. He lunges for it with such speed, I assume it isn't his own. It drops near the couch. I try to grab it before he can, but he's too fast.

You've been thorough at clearing signs you've ever been here. My brother pauses. Does he get a whiff of your used condom down there, even though it is gone? He struggles to stand, some ache due to early morning brittleness. I help him up. When our hands touch, we're both startled. His fingers are as dirty as the credit card in his pocket.

Before I can ask him what he wants, he's already in the kitchen where the tulip-shaped vase is upside down waiting to dry. He looks for a figure, nothing more. He doesn't even step too far inside the kitchen, just checks to see if anyone else is around.

He doesn't go into the bedroom. It's for the best, since the drawers are in disarray to help hide Leyli's loot. My brother probably doesn't want to see anything he'd have to react to, not this early.

He looks at the moths on the living room wall, at least seventeen of them.

"You been here before?" I ask.

"Once, when I brought Uncle from the airport. I had to call him to get the address again."

"And?"

It's my way of asking what he needs. He scratches his ear from some abrupt itch. The sudden movement scares me. I jump back as if he's going to strike me. I immediately regret showing signs of wariness. I hate having a reaction outside of my control, but perhaps it's better to cower and protect my face.

"I thought she'd be here," he says.

"Who?"

"Mom. She's missing again." He says it with was such frustration, I immediately feel guilty.

"Again?" He can tell I'm confused. It's all news to me.

"I forgot. You weren't around the last time."

He means it as an insult, and it works.

"She's not here."

Something in him bubbles. His body inflates with some energy that wasn't there when he arrived.

"You never know," he says. "Maybe in her state, she forgot that you weren't around. Might have mistaken you for dutiful."

"We can't all take your lead."

He stops himself from responding. A syllable forms in his mouth, but he drops it. He's taking steps to control his rage. His fingers might be dirty, but his knuckles aren't worn away.

It's an awkward feeling being near the person who attacked me a mere few months ago. I can blame it on the harsh comedown after his drugs, but I know there's an ember in him that might ignite again.

"You know what they say about you?" my brother said the night he beat me. "You know what I've heard?"

He was seething from the aftermath of meth, jolting himself in surprise with each move. But he kept on and I let him. I like to think we're equally matched in build. If he had to carry boxes of mannequins to my father's shop, I carried the same, even though we looked at different ones in longing. But he threw me to the floor and kicked me, and then ran to get a knife. My mom just watched. She didn't say anything. If my dad were around, he probably would have fetched the knife to slit my throat too. Did my brother plan on stabbing me? At a certain point, I sat up. I walked to the door. My brother started vomiting on the dresser. He splattered his guts on the wedding portrait my mother moved around, not out of any sentimentality for her marriage, but to keep the wound fresh.

I want to ask him what he did after that particular fight. I ran away and I found you. You helped me clean the blood from the corners of my eyes and stroked my eyelashes with the care of a painter cleaning his best set of brushes. But my brother, did he go home to weep or just march right back out for another purchase?

My brother opens his mouth real wide and shifts his jaw until it cracks. "I always hoped you'd be the one to take care of Mom if anything happened. I hoped something would make you take some responsibility in this family." He assumed a feminine boy wouldn't venture too far from his mother. In some ways, I hadn't. "You know where she might be?" His way of asking if I'll help.

"I have some ideas."

He nods with almost imperceptible gratitude.

"Here." He tosses me a pack of unopened gum. Grape. A flavor he hates. Must have suspected I'd be around, since I preferred it when I was a kid. Or this early, buying a pack of his brand of cigarettes, he probably grabbed something extra to round out the cost.

15

My mom studied classical literature but stopped her dissertation before getting married. I thought it was my fault she quit going to school, that I was the rift that made her life into before and after. Later I had more sense to realize it was the revolution, for which her feelings, as for many, were complex.

When I was younger, she always traveled with a stack of index cards tied with ribbon. As my reward for behaving while she dug around in the stacks, she would give me pistachio nougat candies. She looked up descriptions of Medusa, about her two immortal sisters, Stheno and Euryale, her rape by Poseidon, and her beheading by Perseus. I always was bewitched by Medusa.

"Of course," my mother would say. "It's what the Gorgon wants."

My mom was so insistent on telling me about Medusa's mythology, the misconception that she was hideous when she just as well could have been gorgeous. And when my mom finally found a translation of Hélène Cixous's texts, she told me about the laughing Medusa and the horror she brought out in men. But her research always somehow took her back to Ferdowsi's *Shahnameh*, written at the turn of the first millennium. In it, the poet describes a demon king.

"Zahak had snakes on either shoulder," my mom recounted. "They were only tamed after eating human flesh. I'm sure you have a little of him in you."

I thought about Zahak in the Tehran Central Library when, at age eight, I was startled by a big, hard dick poking from the next shelf over. I was too distracted to look at the man's face. His cock was three chapbooks wide. For a moment, I felt jealous for never having learned to play the flute.

The man said, "Go ahead and memorize it."

So I did. For a week, whenever alone, I would draw his dick, just to make sure I remembered it in case I was asked to prove my memory. I drew it with honey at breakfast on lavash. I drew it with my strand of hair in the sink. I drew it with a pen on my hip where no one else would see. I wondered if during future sexual encounters I would see the same dick, discolored at its base. But every time I met new men, even when I didn't see their faces in public toilets, I wondered if I would see the dick that I was asked to recall.

I look for my mom on all eight floors of the Tehran Central Library. She isn't near the poetry, or strolling in Ebn Sina Hall. She isn't near the archival books, even though translated Nordic mythology was on her list. She isn't looking up articles in *Shokufeh*, the feminist newsletter from a century ago.

On the bottom floor of the library, a young woman cuts old handouts into scratch paper. Children run down the conference room smacking each other with Saadi's master-work. I pass a shelf of books in envelopes held on reserve. I hear my mother's voice. Not loud, but still unmistakable.

"Wasn't it Hesiod that spoke of Demeter's snake?"

I stumble onto a private conversation between her and herself in a paradise of columns she's made of books. She flips through texts with velvet covers. Piles of books surround her, all on the subject of snakes, from cookbooks on how to cook reptiles to the pages from *Atharva Veda*. She has brought her own battery-operated fan that swivels left and right. Open books weigh down other open books. She uses her hands to keep the top pages from moving unless she wants them to.

She tilts her head in my direction, but doesn't move her eyes.

"I'll be done with this aisle in a moment." She points to a page. "I hope to someday see the Agora of Areopagus, the plaque of the Queen of Snakes."

My disappearing mother doesn't remember who I am, but has memorized in fine detail the research she did before her marriage. I rub my chin, an anxious tic.

"We have to go now," I say to her.

She has no intention of getting up. In her mind, I'm a stranger interrupting her research. I'm sure others huff when she takes over the library stacks by splaying her finds around her on the carpet.

I can earn her trust through the route of distraction. Typically, dried figs in a napkin are enough. I make sure to arrive with some, since they're complicated to eat. When the skin sticks to napkin paper, she has more to do than wonder who I am.

"Care for some?" I ask. "These were my mother's favorites."

It feels like I'm quizzing her with the hope that she'll snap out of her trance. I ran away after her accident and refused to take part in the aftermath. Better to leave the official diagnosis for someone else, a riddle that became my brother's to unfold.

"Is everything okay over here?" a librarian with a slight lisp asks. I expect her to toughen up and demand my mom leave. "Nilofar, dear, is everything all right?" She uses her name with such familiarity, I realize I'm the stranger they're both annoyed with.

I think fast. "I was looking up a book about the Shahmaran, the King of Snakes."

My mom perks up.

"No, dear." She stands with difficulty, since she's been sitting cross-legged for hours. "The Shahmaran was the *Queen* of Snakes. A young man fell into a cavern while looking for wild honey and he landed in a kingdom of snakes, where he began an affair with the queen."

I remember the tale from the *Arabian Nights*. The traveler and the Queen of Snakes live together for years until he misses his family. They reluctantly part ways with the condition that he is to keep her kingdom a secret, otherwise it will mean her death.

The librarian returns to her post. My mother continues her tale.

"The traveler returned to his family where he learned his local king was sick. Feasting on the Queen of Snakes was the only cure for the king's ailment. Not realizing he was being followed, the young man returned to the cave to warn his lover that the royal army was coming for her. They spent another night together. Upon his leaving, the Snake Queen told her lover a secret. 'Eat from my head, and you will live forever. Eat from my heart, and you will die.' Unbeknownst to the traveler, a royal officer overheard their conversation. The army barricaded and killed the queen. To the king the greedy officer fed the Snake Queen's heart, taking her head for himself to attain eternal life. But the clever Queen of Snakes had lied. It was he who ate her heart that would live forever."

My mother thinks about the story deeply for some time before snapping out of thought.

"Khosh amadi." With formality, she says she's glad I came. "What's that you got there?" She motions to the figs. I hand them over. "Thank you. I prefer them fresh." Did she always? I never considered that her taste might change after her concussion. "Growing up in the rose fields of Qamsar, I wrapped fresh figs in too large a cloth. It always deceived me into thinking I had packed more than I actually did."

"It's a wonder you were named Nilofar. Why water lily and not rose?"

As expected, she peels the paper from the figs.

91

"I grew up in a town mad with roses: boiling, bottling, and packaging them. It was bad luck to name your daughter after the main export."

My mother always looked like a Botticelli maiden to me, since her features were lighter than anyone else's in the family. Now all that was silk has dried. Her cheeks are the most obvious. Ashy grayness has replaced what was once rosy. Her scalp rustles under her headscarf from dryness. My brother might make sure she bathes, but he doesn't insist on any extra care.

"Can you take me to the graveyard?" my mother asks. "I like to go early before the sun burns the stones. I like speaking to the grave on my knees. We can learn much from the dead."

The librarian nods to her as we leave. "Nilofar, I found the book on Polygnotus's terra-cotta jar."

"Oh, good!"

The librarian turns to me. "Are you her pupil?"

"I'm her son." The woman is shocked. Clearly, she didn't know Nilofar had any children.

I help my mother into the car. She looks at me closely. From just a dose of hormones, I imagine my hair has softened. Impossible, but perhaps my mother can see a break in time. Can she tell there will be less hair to tweeze out of my ears, or fishbones to pluck from my beard?

She looks at me and says, "When I see your face, I am reminded of the shah's ripe ruby fruit that grew only in his palace stream and died when out in air."

16

"The tombstones are still warm from yesterday's heat," my mother yells.

I stare at a grave marker for a couple—husband and wife—buried one on top of the other. I have no desire to see my father's grave up close to reflect on how things were, before my mother's car accident, my brother's blunt fists, and the knife that almost cut my neck.

A woman approaches me with a basket. "Roses?"

I buy two yellow bouquets swaddled in baby-shower wrapping paper, too thick to be delicate. My mother stands over the grave and washes it with rose water by hand. She uses the bucket we keep in the trunk for these visits. Before his burial, what was the bucket for? Perhaps another death that now, somehow, is less important.

"I wish you had met my husband," she says, referring to my father. "You'd have loved him. I can almost smell his cologne."

The cologne he put on for other women? I want to point out.

After he left for the night to carry on some hardly secret affair, my mother would sit in front of her bedroom mirror and comb her hair with a wooden brush. She would put on lipstick she dug from the back of her drawer behind a box of unused henna. And when she thought she was alone, she would look at herself in a way I feared I would look at myself one day. For her, grief had no easy escape.

The roses don't remain intact for long. My mom tears the petals off the stems and scatters them over my father's grave. While she mourns, I imagine pressing my face into the dirt and yelling until cliffs in Kish crack. Farther off, an old man uses antique scissors to cut thorns off a bush. After finishing one stalk, he removes his hat to catch his own tears.

"Poor man," my mom says. "He's been the cemetery gardener since age thirteen. They fired him last year, but he still comes back daily. Crazy, isn't it?"

A sly gust of wind pushes all the dried flowers off a neighboring grave. Some deep guilt causes me to drop down and save the petals. I cover them with my body. My mother sees it is important to me somehow. She also rushes over and scoops up rose petals to add to the grave.

"Was it someone you knew?" she asks.

"No. But they deserve the company."

Behind her, a figure pauses. A man I suspect might be tailing me. He has a trench coat over his arm and pivots when I turn toward him. I can't tell how seriously to take my paranoia. He climbs across the yard before I know it.

"There is one more grave I'd like to visit," I tell my mother. I find my way there easily.

Memorial stones with Koranic passages rise over my grandmother's plot. Her bones might be below, but I know she'd have preferred being in Qamsar with the roses she always feared the wild deer would eat. My mother never felt guilty for having her mother buried in Tehran.

"She's the only family I have left," my mom insisted. "And graves are for the grieving, not the dead."

Because of the pills, I know I will crave pickled lemons and lick my hands for their salt. I might have looked up their effects once before, when plotting our escape was purely hypothetical. My fingers aren't softer yet. I will eventually purchase gloves in case I stop recognizing my own wrists.

My grandmother after taking too much morphine told me about her other daughter, the one I never knew.

"She met her end in stone." I didn't know what she meant at first, until I found out they called her a whore for sharing a bed with another woman's husband. Her death came from one tossed rock after another. "I didn't know what it meant when I read it in tea."

I tried to change the subject when she brought it up. I didn't want to inherit such a pathetic end. I can't help but think of you here. What bucket would I use to wash your grave?

"Is the tale of the Queen of Snakes from book three of the *Arabian Nights*?" I ask my mother.

"There is no book three to those tales. Various nights. Various chapters. There are editions that cut the book apart so they're fit to travel, but nothing as formal as a separation in the actual work." Near my mom, a garden snake curls. She lifts it and holds it close to her mouth. "Was it you who killed Canopus?"

I take the little thing from her and place it on a pile of leaves. It lies limp before slithering eastward. If I knew where you were, I'd call to tell you all this. I'd dictate the panic that the effects of my mother's concussion, of which we were the cause, will pass on to me. I know it can't, logically. But perhaps by way of all curses, somehow it will.

I deserve it. If we are two pearls, then tragedy will forever be our string. My mother came to the bookstore all those years ago. She was looking for me, or perhaps the copy of *Haft Paykar* I kept mentioning. I was there, and so were you. She dropped a sack of white raspberries. Instinctively, I elbowed your dick away from my face. You quickly zipped yourself up. It was no use. She had seen us.

I chased her to her car. Without looking in my eyes, she shook her head, started the engine. "Sometimes I wish you were dead." Her shock was poetic.

She sped down the block, almost all the way home. With a clumsy turn, she collided with a cantaloupe vendor. It would have been laughable if she hadn't shattered part of her skull. I still can't stomach cantaloupe, not even the smell of it. On our block, the street was slick with melon rind for months.

"At least she isn't paralyzed," the doctor told us. Another failed attempt at solace. But my own logic was far more brutal. At least she'll keep our secret safe.

17

We stop at a corner bread stand. I buy barbari in case my mother has nothing to feed herself at home. The baker digs his hand into the stone oven to drag out bread that's gotten stuck. Since he's the youngest behind the counter, he has something to prove. From the screams, it's obvious he kept his hand in the oven for too long. His cohorts grab a nearby bucket of water, in it a clean rag, and dunk his hand inside. It's too early to tell how bad the burn is.

My mother watches the scene along with me.

"How long can someone stand in a fire of their own making?" I ask. I don't expect a response, but she speaks anyway.

"Queen Dido, for example? According to Marlowe's play, she built the fire she eventually used to kill herself."

"I remember. After her lover left her. Wouldn't someone try their best to escape a fire? Wouldn't a body inherently try to flee?"

"Mythology doesn't exist for realism. Some fires you don't realize you've made." My mom tears off a piece of bread and eats it.

I always pause in front of the building where I grew up. I stop at the swing set adorned with fresh roses around the frame. Even decades ago they were so beautiful, I swallowed as many as I could until I grew sick and vomited out nothing that at any point resembled a flower. I liked to pretend the petals became part of my insides and that at any moment I could sneeze, piss, shit, or jizz a rose.

The apartment is the same as when I moved out. Only the stains on the rug are different, namely a black one I now notice. My dried blood. Now, my nose isn't broken. And now, no one threatens me with a knife. Not yet. The shape, the spilled blood—if I squint, it looks like me.

It'd be easy to hue memories of this place with golden light, especially since the streetlamps on the road feel like they're somehow closer to the building by several feet than they used to be. I know it isn't possible. There has been no new construction on this block. As a teen, I hated how the streetlamps exposed the secrecy of my bedroom with orange bulbs. I won't let myself sentimentalize the pomegranate tree that I climbed too often in order to leave my room. From up high, I could still spot my mom crying because somehow she ended up a housewife with all her essay drafts tucked away. After all that self-sacrifice, her husband left her for someone else.

Once inside her apartment, my mother pulls books out of the oven where she keeps the overflow since there are few shelves left. She finds a copy of *Kalila wa-Dimna* in the icebox. She highlights the tale about the frog king who fed other frogs to a snake.

"He found you?" my brother says to her with concern. She rises when he enters the room as one does for a guest.

"Khosh amadi." She nods. I'm glad you came.

"Mother, would you like some tea with your bread?" I ask.

"Are you taunting me? I am no mother."

I boil water. I put feta and bread on a plate and take it to her. There are no tablecloths in the drawer. In my absence, they've just eaten over the silk rug from Tabriz. On it, a few crumbs. She takes two sugar cubes for her tea. It might be too soon, but I avoid looking directly in the pink plastic mirror above the kitchen sink. I'll notice the difference, that my nose is less angular, that my tongue is less barbed. My brother can tell I'm taking stock of what's missing.

"I had to hock some of the furniture to pay rent."

"Just until I get a grant," my mom says. Her thicker books are organized in one pile, the thin pamphlets sitting alongside the other thin ones. I swallow the bitterness in silence when he shuts her books to clear the table with no care for the page numbers she'll lose.

Dry jasmine flowers sit in damaged teacups around the apartment: next to the television, balanced on the broken thermostat, and under the glass coffee table. They perfume the room from their cracked, worn-away vessels.

"Are the jasmine vines in the garden still growing tall?" I ask my mother.

"I haven't seen any."

"Then where did you pick these from?"

"Those aren't my doing. The other man. He brings them."

It's a surprising show of gentleness. I can't picture my brother collecting flowers.

We once had fine china and glassware from former dynasties. I can't find any of it. My brother must have sold it to keep up his habits. And all the odds and ends my dad displayed in his shop, old hats and canes he carved by hand. I can't find any remnant of him aside from the photos. My brother probably couldn't sell those for meth.

This place has been the stage set for much of our lives. The entrance faces the sliding door to the garden, straight through the living room. The rest of the apartment is a hallway, with the kitchen on the left, followed counterclockwise by: my grandmother's room, my mom's room, the bathroom (at the end of the hallway), my brother's room, and what used to be mine.

The hallway is dark. Depending on the time of day and where the sun is facing, the bedrooms are bursts of light that take several seconds for eyes to adjust to. Behind the linen in a closet, there's a box of tapes. I find an old cassette player in the kitchen drawer and pop in a tape. A crackle. There is no audio, no voices or conversation. I let the static play while I make dinner. Something simple, a pot of rice. My show of gentleness before leaving again.

From the terrace I pictured what it would be like to kill my father like Zahak did in his myth. The young prince was convinced by a sorcerer to dig a pit in which his father would fall. You made sense to me as Zahak. You admitted to having killed your father. You were certain you willed him to have lung cancer after he said you couldn't see me anymore.

"Not until I'm dead."

Fortunately, he didn't get his wish.

I dig through a chest of multicolored gel pens for letters I wanted to write but rarely did. Farther down in the box, there are plastic spider rings, feathers, and novelty holograms from a hagiography that to us was nothing more than a fairy book. Three old bottles of cola sit under the bed. Even the ants that found their way in have dehydrated. Kurt Cobain and Iskander the Great. Both are men I've kept posters of, along with Orion and Shah Kong, the ape. My brother has since sold those, torn or burned them too. I look under the bed and am shocked no milk roses sprouted from all the times I pumped my dick between the mattress and the frame. Sure, I'm the one that ends up on all fours, but for practice I had my way with my bed.

There is no gun where I last hid it. Only empty white pill bottles. I administered the meds for my mother after one of her suicide attempts. Even then, she tried to give me a moment of myth.

"The seeds of snakes," she would say to make the experimental antidepressants less terrifying. The seeds of snakes, because we thought pills looked like serpent eggs.

The cassette tape of nothing but static keeps playing while I check the closet in my grandmother's bedroom, long out of use. The clothes that belonged to my dead aunt were rolled, not folded, after her murder. My grandmother kept them in her bedroom while she was alive. Dresses and scarves each had their own small plastic bag, reserved usually for produce. My grandmother continued to add new clothes to this collection, unworn blouses and dresses. These too she decided to roll, not fold.

Since my mother chastised her for stealing plastic bags from the grocer, my grandmother started to wait until I brought home onions or plums, parsley or mulberries from the corner vendor. She'd fish those bags from the garbage to roll scarves she bought. Most had geometric designs, subtle arabesques.

"I never see you wear them," my mom would say suspiciously. My grandmother was too shy to admit she was buying them for her daughter in the afterlife. If she were to visit on one of the holy days of the year, she'd have something lovely to wear.

Once I caught her rolling a blue scarf with a subtle gold thread.

"Geometric designs distract the evil eye," she said. Another of her superstitions.

We both knew the evil eye didn't travel alone.

The mound of clothes in plastic produce bags reaches the hangers on the closet rack. My grandmother's own dresses suffered many wrinkles from having to share the space, but it didn't matter. I'm sure my brother made a killing from selling all those untouched clothes.

On the cassette, there is finally a change in noise. The static cuts out. My mom clears her throat.

"Herodotus knew the benefit of winged snakes. They guard frankincense, which was once precious. If only I could be like Olympias, mother of Iskander, who too slept with serpents. Or Medusa. Each hair is a snake, and each snake is a curse. Some bite outward, but some bite the gorgon's head to find their way back in."

My brother ignores the recording. He's used to hearing her words in a way I'm not. His forehead has smoothed the remains of acne he was once too eager to peel. We're the same height, even though life has made us slouch in different directions. I hunch forward from reading too many books. "Probably from trying to blow yourself," you'd joke.

My brother, however, slouches to one side. His right pocket used to hide his contraband. His pockets are empty but he still leans.

"I gave up looking for the tapes Grandma would play," he says, thinking that's what I'm searching for. "I thought they'd be soothing for Mom to hear."

"The lute music?"

"You remember."

"They weren't tapes. It was a radio station." I look around my grandmother's room for her stereo that had a leaf sticker on the left speaker.

"It's gone," my brother says. He means it about so many things.

The water in the rice pot bubbles over and hisses on the stove. We both hear it down the hallway. I pause the cassette and hurry to the kitchen to stop any growing mess. I always shut the flame instead of turning it down, some habit even though moments later I'll flick a match into the burner again.

My brother watches me add salt to the boiling water. You'd tell me not to be here, that he's as dangerous as any rope on a citron tree. Even in the aftermath, it was difficult for me to view the attack as having come from my brother. It had the edges of a nightmare. The details blurred as the days came and went. It was real, I know. The bruises and the blood. But it is daylight and without my father, grandmother, or my mother as she was, it's hard for me to accept all that has ended.

"Dad's gun. Do you know where it is?" I ask my brother before he leaves the kitchen. He's surprised I remember, or that I'd have the gall to bring it up. But I don't let up. "The gun Mom threatened to kill herself with."

"She would have done it, if I didn't empty out the bullets. I checked daily back then while she was taking a shower. One morning I almost skipped the routine. That was the day she pulled the trigger in front of me."

I don't remember that day at all.

"Why do you think he bought it?" I ask. A stupid question. We both know. In hopes his suicidal wife would do herself in.

"A cowardly escape strategy. At least she's not suicidal anymore, far as I know."

"I wanted to sell it."

"It's gone too." He pauses. Might as well bring up his own outstanding questions. "Remember when dad left?"

"Why?"

He's annoyed I don't respond with a yes or no. "I can't remember the specifics, that's all. I just remember Mom crying. It was the worst sound. I thought people cried like that only over dead bodies in movies. You think we have addiction in our genes?"

Sometimes he asks questions with such obvious answers, I want to laugh. It already has happened to us. Me with men. Him with drugs. I've seen my brother strung out more times than not in the past decade. I remember the most gruesome, sucking the blood out of his veins because he was scared some heroin was slipping out with the red. I don't understand what he wants from me now. Not forgiveness, but to philosophize our rage.

He juggles kumquats with one hand. He does so either unconsciously or to remind me that there was a little pocket of joy in our youth, when we joked because he knew how to juggle and I knew how to make birdcalls. Canaries most of the time, and a nightingale attempt that never panned out.

"Why'd you even learn to juggle?" I ask.

"To distract you when Mom and Dad fought."

"It didn't work."

"Maybe not for long, but it did for a few minutes. Why'd you learn to make birdcalls?"

"For Zal," I say before I can stop myself.

He hasn't heard your name for a while. He probably hoped that I stopped talking to you. He pauses and just says, "Oh."

In the hallway my mom digs through the cupboards.

"Nilofar, dear, do you remember the miracle of roses?" A vague enough question to see what responses she will produce.

She ponders it. "There is the Virgin. She appeared with roses, no?"

"What about snakes?"

"Is it a reference to Saint George and the dragon? There were the serpent-slayers of *The Faerie Queene*. Unless it's a reference to Zahak. But his snakes were a curse, not a miracle. Luristani artwork uses snakes as fertility figures. Perhaps the miracle is birth."

"It has to be a literary reference, one that happens in book three."

My brother grabs his keys from a shelf. He chimes in before heading out.

"Didn't you have a book on mythology? A 3D one? You drew all over it."

"You're right. I did. But it was a kid's book. Didn't have a book three."

"Maybe something in the endnotes."

The book. I think about it for a moment. He could be right. Leyli's party guest. Omid. Drumming on the cover before he ran away.

18

At the Tehran Museum of Contemporary Art, Omid isn't by the Miró, nor is he guarding the emergency exit. I stop briefly at a Bahman Mohassess painting, a stone body with no mouth. A particular moan, yours, echoes even here.

The museum is cluttered with elbows today. Attendees push their way past one another. A man walks around with a plastic cup of fountain soda. When the condensation drips, he wipes it away with the sole of his shoe. I drift through the soggy shapes of all the onlookers. In my frustration everyone becomes transparent.

I turn the corner and see Omid pacing. He has on a blazer and navy slacks. He's too distracted by his own shoe-laces to notice I've been watching him. He circles the paint-ings, not paying attention to men taking flash photos behind him. He's lost in a particular Dubuffet. A painting of an open mouth stares at him while he sits down on a folding chair to inspect his shoes again. One of the laces has faded more than the other.

I let my shadow startle him. He looks up. From his fold-able chair, he jumps. I'm sure others have stopped to talk to security guards, but he panics. Is he scared I might embarrass him by grabbing his crotch?

Omid's dress shirt collar folds up on the right. I reach over to fix it. A habit. He pulls back, nervous about what it means.

"Sorry for leaving the other night," he says.

Instead of talking, I wish he'd just push me to my knees. I could start a parallel history with a new man. But with someone new, I could never achieve our end goal.

"My book," I say. "You took it."

He looks offended that of all the details of the night, it's the book I came to discuss.

"Oh. That. I can bring it to you after work. Is that the only reason you're here?" Is he hoping I might please him by grabbing his crotch?

"You're the one who left abruptly."

"I can't get caught up in something dangerous. Not with my visa."

"There's only so much you can learn from a museum gig. You should broaden your experiences." I do a good job of convincing him to partake. He adjusts himself. "You remember where I live?"

He nods.

"Good." I leave before he can say anything else.

I can start anew with Omid. Could it be so easy? We can live in the heavy flirtation of two who've just met. But as it solidifies, as we spend more time together, the same dangers will appear. Even with him, I'd have to decide what steps to take to keep from being a target. Besides, I doubt his cum tastes as good as yours. Even when you haven't bathed, your cock smells sweet to me.

I don't do much to prepare for Omid, aside from leaving the door unlocked and checking the bedroom to make sure it's still empty. I hear him at the bottom of the stairs. He climbs the first flight decisively. After the second flight, he pauses. The higher he comes, the slower he walks. But my door is open. I've done most of the work for him. He freezes before knocking.

"You have it?" I ask from inside.

He enters the apartment but doesn't close the door. He fumbles with his satchel, behind which he moves like he's hiding a hard-on. I grab the book and leaf through it for anything that stands out.

I stop on the first snake I see. A footnote about Ovid. Book three. An image of Tiresias. The illustration is of three people: an old man, a figure in transition, and a woman. Eventually, Tiresias was the woman who became a man again after striking another two snakes. Later in the myth, Tiresias is asked if love is better as a man or as a woman.

"As a woman," he replies, "the pleasure is far greater."

In fury, Hera strikes him blind.

I remember I am not alone.

"What's it mean?" Omid asks over my shoulder.

"I'm changing. Can't you tell? Right before your eyes."

He thinks it's a cry for help. "Anything I can do?"

"No."

He's disappointed I don't invite him to stay.

"Can I draw you? Please. Before I go."

He checks his shirt collar in case it has folded up again. I realize he isn't embarrassed to be seen by others. He's worried about being judged by me. If only I could be gentler, I think. But instead I wonder what else would make him self-conscious. If I gestured to his teeth like there's something stuck between them? He'd claw at his sideburns if I hinted there were any flakes. I delight in seeing Omid cower. Could I have been so innocent at some point? Seeing him reiterates the truth. I could never be with anyone else. The pleasures would fade. He's much too ordinary for me. Matching socks. A gradient for two.

I gesture to the leather-bound sketchbook in his hand. "Are those yours?"

He flips through outlines of sculptures from some exhibit he swears changed his life. I recognize Cellini's Medusa, and Bernini's too.

"But that only covers half of me," he says of his sketches from Italy.

He beams over his copies of Abbasi's paintings: a Persian courtier with a partridge at his feet; hunters at a delicate stream; two lovers, one with his hand in the other's robe to allow a tiny peek of skin. They could easily be two men. One of them almost looks like me. Omid points it out too.

"I don't think I drew his chest right. You have a medieval robe somewhere?" he jokes. I rummage around, light a joint, and pass it to him. He takes it. "Didn't know you had these here." He shows off his teeth again, Omid with his open mouth. I take off my shirt. I know it makes him uncomfortable. He might have sketched nudes of men and women before, but never of a figure in transition.

"Go ahead. While there's still time."

He pulls charcoal from a plastic bag. As he scrapes the paper—my side, my knee—my limbs hollow. I don't mind. How intently he looks everywhere but in my eyes. It burns somewhat, being looked into. I hope with age I'll lose the emotion, its specificity. Outside the apartment, the elevator opens. Omid fumbles with the sketch pad. He drops it. A crack, he steps on his charcoal. Because of some automatic setting, the elevator opens and closes on every floor on the hour. The stairs are empty except for the steady massacre of moths in the vents. I take off my shoes without undoing the laces. My slacks drop to my feet. While he sketches me, I wonder if he can tell I will have fewer erections soon. I want to ask him to draw me with jewels around my neck, down my thigh, anywhere. When I climax, there will be no pearls. Thanks to the pills, soon I'll never shoot again.

"You have enough charcoal?" I ask. But he's distracted. "Looking for a guest star?"

"Is he here?"

"Do you want him to be?"

A subtle look of disappointment overtakes him when he realizes we are alone.

"No." He answers too quickly. He probably got off on the idea. I can see his precum through his pants. Must have forgotten any underwear. He grabs his broken charcoal, the largest of the cracked pieces, and takes his time drawing my hair. It's difficult to capture, I know. I turn to get up and make him some tea.

"Don't move," he says. "Please. I'm almost done."

"Fine."

I huddle on the floor naked, my back to him. The carpet is warm, the Persian rug my uncle assumes I lock away. There's a long pause before Omid continues to sketch. He squints to contort my body. I know the image well. I can be a daughter of Danaus. I can retell my life in poses from antiquity. Eventually, he exhales. The sketching continues. My body and hers, they are sewn together in black. When he's done, I feel my torso click into place. Omid takes his time wiring out pubes with the charcoal. He pauses. It makes him harder, I can tell.

I swear, my areolas are darkening by the minute. He scrapes the charcoal with his finger so a few flints drop right on the sketch. A car backfires outside, timed right as three black flecks dot my body. Doesn't sound quite like bullets, but close enough to give me the idea. I still need a gun. For safety.

My back to him, I hear it—his hand undoes his belt. It must feel rough lubing himself with charcoal and spit. Sand, stone. He starts jacking off to scenes of his death in my hair. Does Omid picture you crying in the bedroom? With ashen hands, he makes himself cream. His little gasp signals he's finished. Three shots. Three bullets. He hasn't completed my face. Maybe he'll find someone else to attach the rest of the body to. I trace the drops he's spewed on the rug. Like bloodstains, they look like me. There's a redundancy to everywhere my skin touches itself.

Omid pulls his shirt down. He finds a photo between the fridge and the kitchen counter and hands it to me. Inconspicuous. One of our own, a landscape you photographed after a fuck. It's the color that stands out.

"Where was this?"

I shrug. "I can't tell."

"Did you take it?"

"No. Zal did." He doesn't expect to learn your name. "We often hopped in Zal's car to search for particular colors."

I played Cocteau Twins cassettes for the gentle dance on the highway that rattled enough to make us hard. Seeking indigo crops or lapis gas stations, we stayed on the road for this whim of blue. For a week, you were haunted by some invented fruit you never did eat.

"It's blue, even under the skin." You swore you'd had it before.

We looked in markets, but in Yazd they tried to show us weave work and termeh instead.

"What about blue fruit?" you asked a vendor.

He thought about it for a long time. "What color are the pits?"

You paused for the same amount of time. By your expression, I could tell you realized you'd dreamt it all up.

"And where is Zal now?" Omid asks back in the kitchen. He has charcoal on his neck from scratching himself.

"Hah. An ongoing question."

"Sorry about that." He points out a cum stain on my jeans, one of his that snuck through when I put my pants back on. There's also charcoal down the front. "You should soak them so the powder doesn't set."

I head to the closet to swap them out for another pair. I notice that among my clothes, you've added your gray jeans, the ones you wore to and from the hospital. They were hung up hastily, half off the hanger. In the final moments before you left the apartment, you must have realized you should leave these pants behind too. Why would you leave them here if you've removed all other traces of yourself? Because they're my jeans. You made a big deal about me wearing your pants because I always found a way to leave ink stains. Yours were yours and mine were mine. So I wrote my name on the tag. But you were wearing my pants that night. I try not to dwell on the fact.

I put them on and join Omid again. As a thank-you, he puts his fingers through my belt loops and pulls me close to him. "I can't believe the heartache you've been put through." Our crotches touch. Omid kisses me. I let him. His hands dig deep into my back pockets and fish something from the left one. A piece of paper, maybe a gum wrapper.

"This your card?" he jokes.

A receipt. From the night of your attack. Bita's Ice.

"Sure."

"I wonder if fucking someone younger was worth it." It's the most perverse thing Omid will ever say. If squeezing a fuck out of someone new was worth the mess. "Hopefully he won't fall for the same trap twice."

I kiss him for giving me that merciless thought. You might.

19

From outside Bita's Ice, I look for Sumac shoveling blackberry ice cream. Customers must be eager for sweetness on such a putrid night. The whole city smells like spoiled meat. At the front of the line, a young family orders a pint of something. They stash their purchase in a lopsided baby stroller. As boys, we enjoyed the pistachio ice cream my dad sold in his shop alongside other wares. He didn't want to waste cones during some sanctions, so he scooped ice cream directly into my hands. You and I tried to practice palmistry by reading those sticky lines.

When I get closer to the front door of Bita's Ice, I realize it's not someone young working the counter. The owner is a middle-aged man with a sailor's hat. I imagine he has a tattoo of an anchor from his heyday sailing the Caspian. Under him, a tiger-skin carpet sops up any spare water that drips off the ice cream scooper.

One detail stands out. A disproportionate number of men slink their way through the line. When it's their turn to order a cup or cone, they wait for the proprietor to give them a nod of approval before heading through a side door. Is this the portal to the underworld?

I wait in line at the ice cream shop behind a young girl who pulls on her unibrow. After she orders her banana smoothie, it's my turn. I work up the nerve to walk past the counter like the other men do. The owner stands in my way.

"My friend Ali Reza is inside," I say. A common enough name.

"Prove it." He wants some signal, some code that I belong. If only I kept every pube I collected on my cheek.

I hesitate. He points to the door.

Instead of leaving, I stand to the side and stare down at the ice cream flavors to buy myself time. Two men pass me. One of them has a glitter tattoo on his neck, the back half of a dragon. They both suck on green lollipops. The proprietor lets them through. Next in line, another couple of young men. These men have only one lollipop. The ice cream shop owner stops them.

"Come on, buddy," one of the men says. He takes the lollipop from his confidant and sucks it down deep. "Call it a two-for-one special." With that joke, they're good to go.

To enter, I know I must snag a green lollipop. The market next door has them. I buy two and roll them both in my mouth. I make my way to the front of the ice cream counter. The sailor stops scooping raspberry ice and looks me over again. I don't look threatening enough to make him worry, even though I've walked through the line once before.

The green lollipop is my key. The shop owner takes pity on me and lets me through.

I trail down a fluorescent void that smells like vanilla and shit. A door beckons at the end. Plants block the entry to help with discretion. First, I'm met with the hornets of mirror ball light. In an otherwise unremarkable room with two lava lamps, two boom boxes vibrate, one with classical lute music and one with a Googoosh remix. Countless caterpillars in opulent wigs blow hookah smoke in a combination of emojis and arabesques. Someone plays *Super Mario Brothers* on a flickering monitor.

All the picture frames hang with extra-long strings, probably because there are more suitable images on the other side for daytime guests. But for now they are studio portraits of Valentino with dicks drawn on. A window is covered by a long wooden board and a scrap of velvet that has been torn down and restapled innumerable times. Anything to make sure the view is blocked. Ants wander in and out of a random crack growing in the middle of the wall.

It is a trick of light. Every time I look up there are more trees. Judas trees, lindens. Some of the men eat snow cones. Morning glories grow between them. I imagine others turn to trees themselves. Silver birches and European elms. Men inhale the cigarettes while others blow out the smoke. I try not to let it overtake me, the disgust, not that these men rub up on other men, but because they've done so while I've been trying not to. I'm usually side by side with men averting eye contact, unless I'm on my knees. Perhaps I too am a walking wound of a tree.

"Excuse me," I say to the bartender.

He slides me a drink with a crack on the rim. "Don't touch your mouth to the glass. It'll cut through your gums."

"Was there a raid outside here? Six weeks ago?"

"Six weeks back? And you expect me to remember? Honey, it'd be easier if I told you which days there weren't raids."

I down my drink.

A man in a veil with gold sequins sewn around the edges sings a Shohreh medley. Makeup is spackled on his face and his lips have been pumped with fillers. His dainty nose narrows to a sharp point.

"Sing something modern," someone yells.

He stops in the middle of his solo. "You bitches are too baked to appreciate anything."

After the song, he peels off his veil and tosses it over a barstool. Underneath, he's dressed in a soccer jersey and mesh shorts with heels and painted toenails. He kisses the air in the direction of regulars, and stops in front of me.

"Anjir?"

"Yeah."

He lunges forward to hug me. I stay stiff. He smells sweet, the tail end of several perfume bottles shaken and added to different corners of his skin.

"You don't remember me?"

I squint to let the face reassemble into one I recognize. The image lands once I spot the left side of his lip. In grade school, we taunted a little boy with a birthmark kissing his mouth. Peymon. I remember helping him finish his homework one day. I helped him spell Avicenna's name for a report on the polymath. We spent a weekend with his father decades ago. Most of the time his dad didn't even know what kind of birds he was hunting. He just shot at the whiteness. When the birds fell, he walked over to see his kill.

"A shame," he said of a hawk, as if he wasn't the one who shot it down.

In the club, Peymon raises his eyebrow to suggest he knew I was into men.

"I suspected," he says. "But then again, I suspect so many people, and then I never see them here. I was always curious about you, even though you didn't speak up any time I was bullied."

"I don't remember."

It's a lie. Of course I do. I wasn't effeminate like him, harassed every day. Even I must have pushed him off a carousel to keep the others from noticing my daintiness. Kicking was easier for the other boys. It gave them a chance to practice their soccer moves.

"Don't worry," Peymon says. "I never hold a grudge. In fact, I see all. Classmates and friends and even some teachers."

"Even Zal?"

He grins. "Yes."

"When'd you see him last?"

"You guys have something special?"

"Something especially rotten."

He tries to calculate the answer to my question. "I might have seen him a few times. But not after the last bust. Four people were beaten and the rest of us hid in the freezer until it was safe. I almost froze my nuts off. Did you hear about the man in the news? The one they hanged from a tree?"

"In passing." Another lie.

"Tough way to go. I was arrested once." He raises his shirt to show me his back. Some of the wounds look freshly spewed, even though they've dried. "I have to keep them greased so they don't hurt. One hundred lashes. Sounds so old world. But they counted out every single strike. It really is different being made to drink from a dog bowl by a prison guard, more erotic than performing for a lover. Stickier. Somehow always wet."

"Thank God you're alive," I say.

"It was my first offense. The guy they hanged, it was his third. But what else can we do?" Peymon knocks back a drink. He focuses his eyes on my hair. "You look a little different."

"Do I?" It's subtle at this point, my own doing. My hair is longer. I skipped the last haircut.

"You look a little more feminine, if you ask me."

"Just you wait." He doesn't know how to react to my comment. I turn to my cup to keep from noticing.

"Good for you. If it's what you want. Me? I never could. But I haven't been in love." He reapplies his lipstick in wide strokes.

"I'm not sure love is enough."

He smiles. "It'll have to be."

"Sometimes I wonder what difference it makes. Couldn't I just wear a veil and pretend like we were man and wife?"

"You'd think so, but they'll know. They check when you're arrested. It's the ones who haven't gotten the surgery that get the worst of it. They make less sense to the devout. My dear, even if it all goes swimmingly, even if you transition and get all the stamps on all the forms, the brutal truth is this: Society might not be accepting. I know of at least a dozen who've still been arrested after surgery. The police might hassle you anyway and book you as a sex worker. Or violate your body because they think rape doesn't compare to the violence you've inflicted on yourself. It'll still be difficult."

I know. Transitioning isn't a cosmic change that will make everything simpler. We build our own narratives of ascension. I fumble with the old receipt for Bita's Ice. "Zal was here with someone. I was hoping to find him."

"Hold up." Peymon approaches the bartender. Peymon gestures for him to come in closer. They touch cheeks. Peymon whispers something to him. The bartender looks me over, then whispers a response. Peymon leans over the counter, his heels off the ground to grab something. He hands me an empty three-gallon ice cream pail. The outside is glossy, even though the insides have been wiped clean. The lost-and-found pail is mostly full of bobby pins. Neon green condoms litter the bottom, two halfway out of their wrappers. There's a pipe. A tube of black lipstick is missing its cap. There's also a coin purse (empty) and a wallet. I open the Velcro and see the school ID of a young man.

"I don't know much about him," Peymon says. "But I haven't seen him since that night."

Your new love. The tail end of eighteen. From Sumac's wallet, I hold up a card with his address as if it'll unlock some secret. How much do I care to know about him? And does it matter at this point? It does. I don't want it to but it does. Otherwise, I will always worry that I went through this for the wrong reasons. To keep living, yes. To be with you.

"Will you come again?" Peymon asks before I leave.

"Maybe."

I rub his back when I say goodbye. It's part apology, and part act of sadism. I wonder if I can still cause him pain.

"You make me sick," I said to him when we were kids.

Those obscenities bent backward, whether I knew it or not.

I pause by the freezers. I listen to their hum, loud enough to drown out any music, now an Erasure beat. For a full two minutes, I'm okay with not breathing.

Outside Bita's Ice, a young kid eats his chocolate ice cream, and his mother downs a watermelon smoothie. They smile where you had your breath kicked away. There is no use cursing the children who play hopscotch where the men cracked open your bottom lip. It's the same stage set, but these kids don't know. They might experience savagery of their own,

gagging on the steam off a frontal lobe, the bashed head of a
schoolyard friend for some stupid reason: too deep a V-neck,
a CD player in public. Still, I want you by my side to sit with
me in the fracture we've yet to seal.

20

A woman finishes taking her laundry off a line, bedsheets of different sizes with the same rabbit embroideries around the edges. She wipes her sweat with the corner of one of the blankets. I follow her inside a building that tapers on its way up. There are three apartments on each floor. Number 3, the same as Sumac's ID.

"Is this where Agha Daryoosh lives?" I call out to the woman as she starts up the stairs.

She drops a heavy wicker basket from her shoulders. She gives me a once-over and pulls her chador tight.

"The young man or the elder?"

For some reason I think asking for his father would be less alarming.

"The father. Is he in?"

"He's probably at work." I look at her blankly for any answer to my question. She sighs. "The Tehran Zoo. Kooy-e-Eram."

"Of course." She hoists up her laundry to hurry out of the conversation. "And his wife?"

Irritated, she drops her laundry down again. "What about her?"

"Is she home?"

She examines me closely. "You really don't know the family too well, do you?"

"I went to school—"

She interrupts. Clearly, she doesn't care.

"Long gone, far as we know." Before leaving, she looks at me intently to make sure I have no more questions. "Is that all?" I nod. "You know, you kinda look like the kid."

"Do I?"

"It could just be the shadows." The woman continues up the stairs. "You should go see his room before it's gone."

"Will it disappear?"

"It just might. I'm told the young man ran away."

A vine outside the apartment hallway window twists ever so slightly through the hinges of the front door. The bold wisteria wants to sneak in as badly as I do. I touch the tip with my finger before wrapping it around my thumb to yank. With the pull, part of the paint from the frame pops off. The door is easy to unlock.

In the fridge, there is little. Soccer ball magnets on the door hold up photos of Sumac as a boy. Him standing with a fishing line. Him in mustard overalls. A photo booth strip with a green-screen Eiffel Tower behind him. Pink and beautiful as if nothing could ever tear or harm his skin. Not like mine, already from pink to gray. His father's room is too clean. I don't have the stomach to open his Koran to see what passage he keeps rereading.

I enter Sumac's room. For some reason, I expect him to be waiting for me, splayed on the bed like he's anticipating being fucked by one of his many men. I would have my way with him if I had the chance. I shift to keep my stiffness from curving in on itself.

His room stinks of pinkness. Pink candies left under the bed. Spoons stained Antoinette pink from eating cherry rice, and used dental floss colored pink from strawberry Coke. The bed was obviously made by someone in a rush. The sheets under the comforter are still scrunched rather than pulled taut. The wrapper of a green lollipop crinkles on the floor.

Perhaps the boy has a stash of porn somewhere, like I did with the outdated laptop I kept under my bed, one with seven keyboard keys that didn't work. In a folder within a folder, I saved images and videos before sites were hidden. And the screen was so battered, at times the videos just expanded in extreme close-ups. A chin could pass for a thigh.

I look under his mattress for smut, the stupidest, most obvious place to hide it. Nothing. He probably doesn't need porn. With supple lips like his, he probably finds action wherever he goes.

When given a stolen moment in his room, I can't decide what would be the most impactful items to steal. If only I'd made a list. A shirt, perhaps. But if I don't know which is his favorite, then what purpose could it serve to wear? A dirty shirt, one crumpled on the floor with striations under the pits. I take it. And his hairbrush. That'll do too. I want to ask if he is in love with you, Zal, if he has seen you often, or if it was the first time.

On his wall, he has posters of Kiarostami movies, ones I loved, but you hated.

"I'm sick of olive trees and Persian films," you'd say.

In a book caught between the wall and his bed, some Rumi collection, there is a photo. It's him, I assume, with someone else. The top half of the photo has been torn off to keep some sort of privacy, the intimacy only a mutual beheading could achieve.

A dirty T-shirt with deodorant stains in the pits. His hairbrush. And from his hamper, I grab some boxers starched with months-old jizz. On the comforter, I lay out his shirt. Next, his underwear. Some dirty socks. Headless, he comes alive.

"You can ask three questions," Sumac says, without a face.

Did you love him? Did he love you? Did you think about me?

His answer is the same for all three: "Only when we laughed."

I tighten the bulb of the night-light to make sure it never loosens. Hanging from his doorknob, a necklace sways. Blue glass beads. Not unlike the ones you always keep in your car. Like yours, the beads have morphed from being in the cup holder for too many hot days. It hits me. You've given him a similar invitation. I imagine an arrow through my throat because you might not be done with him yet.

21

The zoo where Sumac's father works is still open. A crowd gathers up front. News reporters tell of an arsonist who set fire to some of the birdcages. Employees check on surviving peacocks to make sure they haven't swallowed too much ash. The snipes huddle in a corner to sleep.

"He started at the parrot cages," a man tells a woman.

A double-decker bus parallel parks. The tourists inside point up at a flame in the night, perhaps an owl set ablaze.

"And he just ran off?" a woman asks another.

There's nothing left for the firemen to do since the last fire extinguished itself. The gull disappeared into the exquisite blankness of smoke. Kids step over gelatinous stains trying to guess what burned where. Teens stand in wide circles around each cage to see how other animals react. Only the koalas show concern.

I look for Sumac's father. Just to ask. That's all. Just to see if he knows where his son is now. If he bought himself a set of new luggage with cheap wheels.

"Agha Daryoosh?" I ask a worker deflating pastel pink balloons he couldn't sell during open hours. He nods to another man in black coveralls with two spray bottles tucked into his pockets.

The janitor yawns and shows off his missing teeth, three up top, and one down below. I watch him from afar. Cameras keep flashing, but he sweeps piles of popcorn into a tuft unfazed. He slows every so often as if the thought of burning birds overtakes, while polishing the bars that hide the zebras, or the barricades that keep the soot-covered pelicans in place. Sumac's father sits. I approach him.

"Agha Daryoosh. Can we talk for a minute?"

"You men don't leave well enough alone." I join him on the bench with a map of the zoo folded over the seat. "I don't know anything else about the fires."

"I'm here to ask about your son."

He looks at me suspiciously. "You a reporter or a policeman?"

"Neither."

"Because he was mugged. That's what it was." We both stand.

"Do you know where he is now?"

"How do you know my son?" I can't settle on a lie. That we worked together? That I volunteered at his high school? "Were you with him that night?"

I hold out the photo taken from his room, of Sumac and another man, probably you, taken in any sort of garden. Only the trunks of the palm trees are apparent, and the two bodies with their heads scissored off.

"You." He points at the photo. "It's you, isn't it? You were the one they found him with."

"No. I promise."

There is a change in his demeanor. There is a growing curl of violence.

"You were with him that night, weren't you? It was a misunderstanding, wasn't it? What did he say?" Agha Daryoosh can tell himself it was an accident, that they mistook his boy for someone else, but it won't change the fact that his son is a fag. He steps closer and chooses my shoulders as the place to rest his ashen hands. "It's men like you who put the thought in his head." He hugs me too tightly for me to struggle, as if he needs a figure to lean on to process the thought. If he yelled, I might shrug away from him. But he weeps so softly, the trance is earned. "Because of you, he's dead." He cries two tears into my ear.

"He's what?"

"Dead, dead, dead."

Of course he is. All the blood on your shirt.

Please, I want to beg him. Choke me until you've pushed out my last bit of breath. Always, my mind goes to violence. On some level, perhaps this is all my fault. If I planned for us to leave sooner, then you might not have looked for others to fuck, others to take down to the strobe with two mismatched stereos, the one in the east playing music from the west, and the one facing west playing Persian cassettes.

The realization hits that I've outlived Sumac, and as a result I've won you. In a way, I know I've lost because I can't ask Sumac how you are as a lover with someone new. The doctors must have told you when you came to that Sumac was dead. He probably still had green on his teeth.

Sumac's father lets go of me and huddles against a hyena cage to weep. Through his tears, he fixates on the rim of a garbage can wet from the remains of discarded cola cups. He sprays the wastebasket and scrapes the sides with his nail, something to do, using a cotton towel as a layer for indirect touch.

Ours is a love that knocks all the peaches off trees. Ours is a love that leaves other lovers dead. All your tears make sense to me now. Because you were caught. Because of you, a young man was killed. I can't pretend to feel sorry for him. I do and I don't. His death is another bead that we tick further down the prayer necklace. There is hope for our pact.

22

No answer after several knocks. Leyli's door swings open with one of the master keys. All the curtains are drawn.

"Well, well, well," she says. She's more bruise than human being. "Aren't you a sight for sore thighs."

She's removed everything from the surfaces of the nightstands and dressers, including the television and the phone. Even the mattress has been pushed off the box frame, but the bed skirt remains in place. The lamps lean against the walls. She looks different without romantics puffing out pleasantries, name-dropping philosophers and minimalist composers. None of the art is on the walls, perhaps a way to ward off claustrophobia. On her bed, there's a photo of a man onstage holding peonies and sheet music. Years back, Leyli as she once appeared.

She looks across the roughage for her cigarette case. "I wanted a birth like Venus. I wanted to enter the world out of a shell." I change the water in a vase of oleanders, though it won't help. They're all dead. "Everyone said I'd make a beautiful woman. But look at me. I'm hideous."

"You aren't hideous. You're only seeing in-between." It's the bruises, I tell her. "You probably envisioned yourself at a gala, not wheezing into paper bags until pain meds kick in."

"Why are you here?" She isn't in the mood to receive any visitors, or to even fake being kind. "This isn't a peep show."

I hesitate to tell her the reason, but there's nothing else to say.

"Your pills. I'm here for more."

She tries to process the information. When it clicks, her eyes and lips narrow. "So you're the thief?"

"I'm sorry."

"I'm surprised you haven't been able to find estrogen pills from one of your sources."

"I have no sources. Every drug I own was stolen from suitcases by chance."

"You could go to a doctor. Ask for them by name."

"I can't."

"Why?"

"I wouldn't want them to know."

This offends her on some personal level. She hobbles into her bathroom and returns with ammo.

"Take them. Take them all!" She throws the orange prescription bottles at me. They smack against my chest with varying intensity, depending on where the pills settle in the plastic. "I'd love to see what kind of a woman a misogynist like you would make."

"I don't hate women. I just fuck men."

"That doesn't make you exempt. I sense it in your gestures and in your tone. You want to take the pills for free? You'll have to sing for your supper."

"Maybe there was something about my mother I hated. Not because of her sex, I don't think. Because of how pathetically she stayed in her circumstance. She never contemplated leaving my father."

"Yes?" She's surprised I'm opening up.

"Whenever my father or brother got violent with me, she did nothing to protect me. She let them beat me, she let them send me away. So any idea of a unique love for my mother, this hope for reconciliation, it doesn't exist. I expect nothingness from her. Now nothingness is all I'll get."

"You can't blame her for not knowing the words."

"Bullshit. I can sympathize, sure. But she could have tried harder. She should have. My grandmother didn't know the words, but there was grace in her silences." Leyli expects me to cry, but I don't. "It doesn't help that Zal is imperfect too."

She softens against her will. "Dear, I don't know what you're hoping to get. There are others with tamer relationships. Circumstance has a hand in it, but you've chosen to make it work with him."

"I hated all the examples I've been given. So much grief."

"Then be something more."

"Like you?"

"I'm far too complex to serve as anyone's example." I gather the pill bottles and set them on her dresser. "Take them all," she says. "I don't care."

"You're quitting cold turkey?"

"Pills are kids' stuff. I'm a needles gal now."

"Injections?"

She nods. "The hormones have given me an unfair advantage. Any countertenor should be so lucky."

"What was the process like for you?"

She wasn't expecting to discuss her transition so openly. There's a moment when she decides to either be offended or to actually take pity on me. She chooses the latter.

"In this country it is a labyrinth with many Minotaurs. You can start from several routes, but for public funding, you always end up pleading your case to various panels. Can take months to convince 'specialists' you've always been transgender. They ask all sorts of silly questions to see if you're feminine enough. Where on your body do you spray perfume? How do you hold a knife? How do you stir sugar in your tea?"

"Was your interview difficult?"

"I decided not to get funding from the government. Just used up my own savings. I'm more of an 'ask for forgiveness later' gal anyway. How can they withhold my new papers when they get a load of my new slit?"

"Will you stay in Iran?" I ask her.

"I haven't done away with the possibility. Days go by, weeks, when I think Tehran is improving, that the old order is softening. Then the morality police unloads in front of Sepehr Tower and grabs girls with scarves that are too thin, boys with pants that are too tight." She shakes her head. "It doesn't get easier when one becomes a woman. Death still comes for us all."

She helps me pile her pill bottles. My reflection asks the question I'm too afraid to expose to air. If our love didn't hurt, would I still want it?

Leyli hisses from too much movement.

"Are you okay?" I ask.

She nods. "I can't wait until I can piss without feeling like a blowhole." She laughs first, so I join. "Leyli, oh Leyli," she says to herself. "What have you done?"

"In the folktale, doesn't Majnun go mad after the death of his lover Leyli? Who was your Majnun?"

She laughs. "Majnun was me. My name before. I became Leyli because she was the beloved I always wanted to be. And what will your name be?"

"I don't know. I've never even put on any makeup." Leyli digs through her bag of tricks. She uncaps her lipstick and tests the color on her wrist. She asks what's on my mind. "I'm so deep down in it, I don't know what to do. I don't want to die."

"Naturally." Leyli finds eyeliner and mascara. She holds them up to the light then puts them away. One swab of color is enough. "You're like a child holding on to a broken mirror because he likes his reflection. You don't realize the cut is making you bleed to death."

Leyli takes a napkin and wipes the lipstick from her wrist.

Even though she avoids standing from the pain, Leyli nods her head for me to come closer. She pushes the tube of lipstick on me, ever so slightly, so only a touch of color rubs on my lips.

"You like?" she asks when I look at her nails.

I nod. "What's it called? Jungle red?" She laughs at the reference to the movie *The Women*.

"Let's hope like Joan Crawford I die a bitch." She gently moves my face from one side to the next to catch a bit of light from the lamp sitting on the floor. I'll be back in this room after she leaves to see if I can read her fortune in the way her hair dryer cord folds over itself, or in her lipstick stains on a scrap of toilet paper.

I'm startled by my cell phone. It vibrates. I don't recognize the number, but I still answer.

"Hello?" Nobody responds.

"Is everything okay?" Leyli asks.

I step outside of her room and close the door. In the hallway I listen for any noises on the other end of the line. Nightingales chirp in the background.

"Hello?"

I hear her breathe. After another beat, she hangs up. I know it's her. Pills can be pearls. Bullets can be teeth. Before turning back to Leyli's room, I swear I catch someone in an overcoat peeking around the corner.

"Wait," I call out.

He hurries, I hurry. He runs. I do the same. He turns, I turn. He rushes to the elevator so quickly, the rug bunches with his steps. He slams into the wall as the elevator doors close. I look up to see what floor he stops on. Two. I run down the stairs. I have to try. I make it to the second floor to the wide-open doors of an empty elevator. No sign of him, just the faint smell of cloves. While I'm inside, the elevator is summoned down to the lobby. I ride with it. The doors open to a ferocious amount of light. Someone puts his hand on my shoulder. Before I can focus on his face, before my eyes adjust, he says my name.

"Anjir?"

I recognize the voice. I greet him by way of a nod. Whoever followed me is gone again.

23

My uncle doesn't take off his sunglasses when he says hello. I've foiled his plan to come and go without any family members noticing. The flight to and from Tehran is usually timed so he'd be back in Los Angeles before any jet lag sets in.

Only half of my uncle's hairline is receding. Every so often, a breeze bullies his comb-over in the opposite direction, an unflattering switch he tries to avoid by using scalp cement.

"Your hair is longer," he says, almost like he's heard my thoughts.

"You in Iran to visit your mother's grave?" I know he isn't. He hasn't been to the cemetery once since her death.

"Of course." A lie.

He scrunches his face distastefully when a man from the cleaning crew passes. His smile reappears around the chambermaids and bellboys and sous-chefs, young, cream-colored, several shades lighter than me.

"I thought you weren't working today," he says.

"Just came to pick something up."

"Good. Then you can come with me to the bazaar."

One lie deserves another. "I'd love to."

My uncle has rented a brand-new car, some electric monstrosity that makes U-turns on its own with the press of a button. Dramatic purple and green lights flicker on the dash.

"I wish you'd have told me you were flying in," I say. "I'd have cleaned your apartment."

"No need. I head back to the airport tonight."

"So soon?" I'm not surprised. He rarely stays for more than a day, the amount of time it takes to make sure his offshore bank transfers go through.

"Are you still studying?" he asks.

"I read."

"My sons too. Always reading. Every Tom Clancy."

"Lately, I've been reading Virginia Woolf. From her first novel to her last."

"Oh. Her. I've been meaning to—"

"In her first novel, *The Voyage Out*, Mr. and Mrs. Dalloway appear. That's a full decade before Clarissa got her own book."

"Is that so?" He doesn't know what else to say to me. "I forgot to bring home movies this year. But I'll try to email you footage."

Growing up, he always sent videos of his family, sons I hope never to meet, showing off their convertibles and expensive shoes. They kept touting that their house had an escalator. My brother used to sit and watch our cousins build model cars, and show off their swimming pools. He'd replay the DVDs until they started to skip.

"Some people have all the luck," my brother would mumble while pausing on close-ups of their framed basketball jerseys. If we were fortunate, my uncle would drop off bags of his kids' old clothes, always too small since they were younger than us. And he'd bring us their ratty shoes, sometimes without the laces since he figured we could get those ourselves.

I considered running away to America for a while. I applied to colleges abroad back when I thought I had an aptitude for classical studies like my mother. My uncle is the reason why I have no interest now. Leaving didn't make him seem any less sad. And working at the hotel, seeing people from elsewhere visit, the Americans are every bit as melancholy as anyone else. Perhaps they flaunt different fashions, but they flash the same sense of longing. Being so far from his family seemed more of a burden to my uncle than a relief.

"How big is your library again?" I ask him.

"Well . . . it's still under construction." I know they don't have a library, even though there are two game rooms. "Maybe you can help me out. I need real nice rugs, the fanciest weave work. Money is no worry. Might as well give these sorry so-and-sos my business. Shit." I feel the rumble while he makes a dramatic turn. A flat tire. "Fucking country." He says it like it's the country's fault he hit a pothole. He takes a beat to decide how to react. I hop out without thinking.

Two men pull over immediately. "You need help?" one of them asks.

My uncle checks his wallet for cash to pay for their services.

"Thanks, but no." I wave them away.

My uncle is shocked. "I have plenty of bills."

"Pop the trunk," I say.

"Really?"

While I change the tire, kids collect burnt feathers on the landscape from the plumes of honey birds I'll never see. For ceremony, I tuck your blue glass beads in my shirt. Stolen from Sumac, now they're mine.

At the entrance of the Grand Bazaar, a man carries his wares on his back, pots roped together. His wife unties a bushel of dried hyacinths. I take my uncle through the masses to the rug quarter, past the vendors with an appetite for bronze, and the barrels of pistachios, barberries, and almonds. Overwhelmed by the crowd, he freezes. The bazaar makes my uncle realize that he isn't automatically better than anyone because he's rich. The crowd brings out his fragility, especially when mercantile wagons don't pause for him to pass.

"The nerve," he says of someone swinging a crate of pistachios so people clear out of the way.

"It's all right," I say. "Here, you only matter when you decide to buy something."

I guide him through myrrh and yards of cinnamon bark. A kid with a smoker's voice sells miniature apples and posters of speed racing stars. His sister strings together dried olives with slow elegance. My uncle picks the first rug shop in the quarter. The store owner finishes his midway prayer.

"Welcome." He grabs my uncle's hand and gestures for him to sit down for tea. "We must catch up, my old friend," he says, even though they've never met.

I leave my uncle with him and pass a store selling thousands of evil-eye amulets. The glass pupils follow me through the corridors as I head toward the specialty jewelers. I pause at a shop with a large banner of the Tehran skyline. A giant falcon was drawn in.

The jeweler yawns while repairing two pocket watches. He inspects one before returning to another with a toothpick screwdriver. He shakes his head to ward off sleep.

"Damn thing from Indonesia." He looks up. "What d'you want?" No pretense of formality.

"A gun."

"You a cop or an angry ex-lover? I don't care either way, so long as you have cash." He digs through his stock and offers me several pistols out of a wooden chest. He holds one up to cover his yawn, then arranges three on a satin display case. "They always look better against red. Pick them up. Feel their weight. See which one calls your name. Well, not your name. Let's hope you never use it." His wink is devious. His teeth fillings match two of the three pistols. "You want something larger? Something automatic?"

I pick the most ornate pistol, one with petals poked into the veneer.

"Excellent choice." He demonstrates how to replace bullets, how to lock and unlock the barrel. "How many you want in there to begin with?"

"Three." One for a warning. One for the thigh. One for the forehead. He puts away the rest of the pistols and starts to replenish the rings in the glass display. "Would you take this for payment?" Leyli's string of marquise diamonds.

He whistles in surprise. "Man. I don't have enough change to cover the cost."

"I'll be back for more."

"It's a fine necklace."

"Yeah, meticulously crafted." I hold up the diamonds.

"I meant the one around your neck."

"The beads?"

"I haven't seen any like those, even here, where there are as many colors as cities in the world. But not like that Isfahan blue. You ever been?"

The long and the short of it: "Yes."

In Darband my uncle and I sit at the water's edge. I've been here many times before. My great-uncle died a few miles from here, cleaning his tapestries on the shore. He was washing an abrisham rug by letting the river smooth away any silt. And to agitate, he gently stepped on the submerged rug to help the process. But he slipped and cracked his head on a boulder. The blood tinted the rug before the river took it away several feet. It would make sense that one of our family curses is stone.

The water reflects too much sun on purpose to annoy my uncle. I get a hookah started for him. At this hour, the city hushes with hope no more smog will join the sky. My uncle pushes around his bitter fish and fermented red cabbage.

"I almost had a panic attack back in the bazaar," he says. "It's just . . . it's been so long. I'm used to going to the bank and to the hotel."

"You could have sent one of your sons." A joke. They'd never. "Don't they speak Farsi?"

"I haven't taught them. There's no use." For a second, the briefest of moments, he lets his guard down. Something about the tea, more cardamom than he's used to. "As kids, we'd come here after the Nowruz festivals." My uncle looks out at the mud-covered street. "Tumbleweeds were sold in bundles for people to set on fire. The only bushel I set ablaze made a break for it. Your mom ran after it laughing. It's not like there were any buildings around that could have burned, but in my nervousness I thought somehow the sky would catch fire."

"My mom never celebrated festivals with us."

"Really? It was your aunt's favorite." He pauses because he's never had to call his other sister anyone's aunt. He's never even told his children he had a sibling aside from my mom. He swirls his glass of tea to ward off getting emotional. "Have you ever thrown lotus seeds over your head?"

"No."

"Not even for good luck?"

"I've never tried for good fortune."

"What fortune would you prefer then?"

"Anyone else's."

After our meal, he drives me to his apartment building. I worry about the condition I left it in, even though he says he won't stay for long. There were people in the lobby not too long ago. It's a warmth that's heightened in the elevator, similar to the faint powder smell of our mothers and their first layer of makeup. My uncle and I stop in front of the apartment door. Blood dots the runner on the floor with a single splatter.

"Stay here," I tell him.

I search the hallway for any eyes hidden around any corner, or peeping through holes that weren't there before. Nobody is around, but a threat dangles.

24

The apartment has been ransacked. A knife was dragged down the walls with an exact line across the entire room. Maybe the intruder expected a trapdoor leading to far more damning content. Or maybe the hope was one quick gust of air would split the building in two, the top half tumbling down away from itself.

If only thieves had something better to do than carve into sofa cushions or slash off the hinges of a refrigerator door. But a trail of blood leads to the balcony. Over the ledge, a black cat with fur on half its tail lies on the ground level for a pageant of flies to feast on. Around it, blood swirls a red speech bubble. A comical end. I heave in the corner of the balcony the deepest spit my body lets me spew.

In the bedroom, I dig around for the jewels I stole from Leyli's guests. I toss out the drawers for my hiding spot. It's all gone, the gems and gold, everything except the diamonds I traded for a gun. In place of the stolen trinkets, there's a bubble wrap–lined envelope with a small stack of photos inside. The locations vary—Tochal, Valiasr, Tajrish Bazaar—but they are clearly photos of you and me. Our poses are unremarkable.

Walking, laughing, playing it straight. But I stop at one with a Ferris wheel in view. Outside Eram Park, I am documented on my knees. Before panicking at being seen by a telephoto lens—here, proof—I can't help but admire your expression. I did that. It was because of me. Nothing is more powerful than the pleasure on your face.

Before my uncle joins me in the room, I shove the drawers back. My uncle stands at the entryway with mix of panic and concern. I do my best to keep him from looking over the balcony ledge at the dead cat. I can't handle fanning him until he regains his breath.

"I'm sorry," I grab his arm and swing him away from the bedroom.

"The blood—"

"Everything will be okay." I don't believe it myself. "Trust me. No one is going to ransack your hotel."

"I'm not worried about that."

I crack a joke. "You must be insured."

He doesn't laugh. "What would cause such violence?"

Me, old man. "It's just my luck."

Isfahan isn't too far. Will we be safe there from whoever's been keeping an eye on us? The thought cuts into me like a machete in an apartment wall, a blade through a black cat.

"You should stay at your mom's place."

"Maybe."

"Please." He digs through his pocket for cash. "I don't know what else I can give you." In that moment, I know he feels guilty. He thinks he could have saved me from this life.

"Will you be okay?" It's the stupidest fucking question he could ask.

"Sure."

He looks down at my hair, longer than ever before. "You do look like her. Your aunt."

But I'll be fortunate. I'll escape. We will be lovers, not someone else's cautionary tale.

"It's never easy leaving," my uncle says on the drive to my mom's apartment. "I want to bring my sons so they can see me in a place where they can't poke fun at my accent. Here, I can answer the phone and not second-guess my responses. It's odd owning a hotel, trying to make others feel at home in the home you've left."

He stops in front of my mother's building.

"Come and say hello. My mom would love to see you."

"Next time."

"Yeah. Sure."

My mother peeks out of her window. He drives off without even glancing at her. She opens the front door for me and continues a conversation as if I hadn't left. "Have I told you about the cobra who taunted the Eye Goddess with fire?" I think I see a bloodstain on the back of my mother's head. It seeps through her scarf and spreads.

"Are you bleeding?"

She drops her scarf. "Am I?"

Most of her hair is gone. Her scalp is cut up from razor marks with large chunks of skin gashed out. Nearby a blade soaks in a teacup. In panic I hurry to wipe the blood off her neck and the hair off her shoulders, off her apron and shirt.

"Why'd you do this to yourself?"

"Research. I had to see if the gorgon could shear her own snakes."

Her scalp is so dry, I wince. If I press a scab on her head, I'd feel the exact same pain in the exact same spot. I sit her in the shower on top of a stool to finish shaving the parts she's missed. My hand is good and lathered when I touch her head.

"Does it hurt?" I ask when she flinches.

"No. It's just cold."

I wait for the water in the sink to warm, then relather my hands. She isn't used to being touched by anybody, and I don't have the gentleness for it. I thought I was done being anybody's son.

A time ago, you helped me shave my head to keep them away, those who gawked at me in the street because I was a little effeminate. Better to keep from drawing attention, you insisted. Maybe that's why the knife was held over my head. I left my family before the blood dried on the rug. I came to your house to ask for your help.

"Hello, stranger," I said while you shaved my head.

"Strange hello," you responded.

You tried to clean the blood that had already dried under my eyes with your pinky wrapped in a wet napkin. Some flakes came loose. I couldn't tell where it came from, if there was a slit on my eyebrow that would always sting when I furrowed.

You timed your tears so they fell whenever I closed my eyes. I wanted to wipe the feeling of guilt from your mind. Instead I took longer blinks to offer privacy for your tears.

"What did you do?" you asked like it was intentional. Like I stumbled and fell into my brother's hands moments before he started stabbing the air.

I don't know what I did. But whatever it was, I did it for you. You sat me in the shower and you shaved my head. Now, I do the same with my mother.

"You don't judge me?"

"I don't, Mother."

"Mother?" She laughs. "What a broken word. I owe much to studying mythology. Retellings vary, as do modesties in translation, but everything you ever want to know about human nature has already been spoken."

I wash the edges of the sink. My mother's hair floats around the drain, as do the layers of skin she's removed. With my hair pulled back, she pauses. She grabs something from her bedroom.

"Can you put this on for an old woman?" She holds out a veil, the one she uses to pray. White cotton with red, yellow, blue daisies, and red, yellow, blue ducks. "Please pour me some tea." She gestures to a cold kettle on her dresser.

I try pouring tea from under the veil. I spill. The cloth soaks up the drops.

"Try again." I spill more on her dresser instead of in her chipped teacup. While pouring the tea, the veil keeps slipping. Maybe eventually I'll master balancing cloth on my head, more delicate than practicing with a book. "Again." The pot is empty.

"There was a kid around here named Zal," I say to her. I can't tell exactly what she remembers. "Did you ever meet him?"

My mom snatches the veil off with a magician's sleight. She folds it quickly. From her drawer, she picks out another, this one made of lace. I fold a corner of the fabric in my pocket next to the gun to keep it from falling off my head.

"Yes," she says. "I think I remember the boy." The memory brightens her face. "He was close to one of my sons. They'd sit for hours in front of mirrors as still as they could. I never knew why." Because of my parents' wedding portrait in a round frame. We tried to pose as husband and wife. Quietly we existed in two words. Not. Yet.

I think about my conversation with Leyli. I feel for my mother. She lived between two possibilities. She stayed with a man who wouldn't ever love her enough. She didn't have someone who dared her to escape. Without you, I might be the same. The gate rattles violently. My mother is startled in a way that's familiar. My brother is home.

25

My mom looks around to see what my brother might notice once he enters the apartment. The door to his room is open, like she was digging through it for something lost. She shuts the door before I can look too long at the proof of his bender: paper cups torn apart and piled, mounds of crumpled pages from books he thought taunted him, and shattered porcelain coin banks kids use to collect charity.

"That cruel man," she whispers.

"Isn't he safer now?" I ask.

"Not when he enters with so much noise."

She's right. The smashing of the gate. The slamming of the car door, the front door, the cabinets. His aggression taints the apartment. I stay in my mother's room and observe, partially out of fear, partially to watch his gestures from a distance. He moves frantically, eager to pawn what he can. He stops every so often to flex and release his arm just to make sure his veins are still there. I commit to stillness. Because I'm in a veil, and because my mother's room faces the sunlight, he mistakes me for her. Or he mistakes me for her curtains. He's compromised his peripheral vision for a relapse.

"There's gotta be something," he says to himself while digging through the cupboards for anything to sell. The only gold left comes from the sun, which makes the pillows look metallic, and the coffee table look bronze. He grabs them fooled by light and shoves them in his car. He comes back for more. He cusses when he sees the dirty teacup with the blade my mom used to shave her own head. His grunts cause the knobs on all the doors to ring. I refuse to cower. He throws something.

"All these fucking books," he says of those in the oven.

He mistakes a folio on Cleopatra and her asp for a book-end. He shoves that in his car too, which he turns on before returning to pillage more. It's his chance to take more of her books. There must be a first edition among them.

"Something rare."

"Please," my mom says. She moves out of the corner of her room to vouch for her books. He doesn't care.

"It's payback for everything I've gotten for you."

While he's at it, he remembers the electronics he hasn't sold yet. He dives into the closet next to the bathroom, grabs the cassette player, and tears out a cassette by pulling on the ribbon.

"No," she begs. "Please."

"Leave it," I say from my mother's bedroom. I'm protective of the recordings. They document parts of her we've lost.

After I speak up, my brother finally realizes I am in the apartment too. He peeks his head into her room and sees me there. The veil loosens on my head. He squints to make sure it's me, then commits to his rage.

"What the hell are you doing?"

My brother knocks down a cracked vase, a scare tactic. I don't move. I almost flinch. But I won't, not if this is the last time I'll ever see him. Soon I will be gone. He grabs the veil. He pulls it off my head. With it, a lock of my hair. The gun gets caught on the lace in my pocket. My brother snatches the chador and in doing so pulls the weapon with it. He takes the fabric to the garden, the weight of the gun lost on him even though it alone would be worth selling.

I follow him to take back my weapon. He makes his way down the dark hallway past the bedrooms and the kitchen, into the living room and the sliding door that leads to the courtyard. I catch up with him and wrap the veil around my wrist and fall onto it. The weight makes him drop the fabric. I free the pistol from the lacework and shove it back into my pocket. The movement causes a snag in the veil. My position on the floor makes him laugh. The sores on his mouth echo the sound. He grabs a long lighter for a barbeque that has since been sold. He tries to set the veil on fire.

In the slanted garden, the fire is lopsided. My brother lets go when the flame reaches his sleeve. The cloth shrinks. My brother doesn't swat at the smoke. Instead, he turns back to me. He aims at my face. A fist quakes my teeth. I taste acid as I fall back.

"You deserve it." My brother hits me with the jealousy of a lover because I've betrayed not only him but the image he had of himself. My brother laughs. "You should have seen his face." Even his jitters have jitters.

I sit up and spit out what I can. "Who?"

"I know how much he means to you. I had to ruin it."
He can tell I'm confused. "Zal. I saw him. Outside the ice
cream shop. I knew it was him. I pretended like I didn't, but
I knew it was him. He nodded, I swear, like he was giving
me permission."

"You're lying."

"I was relieved he was with someone else, not my own
brother. But seeing you here now, looking like this, it's sick.
The other guys pinned them down. At least one of the kicks
came from me."

It has to be a trick. He's trying to get a rise out of me.

"He gave me permission." He says it with such serious-
ness, I know he isn't kidding.

It settles in me, what my brother did, the animosity he
aimed at you in order to both protect and pulverize me. We
will be the cause of more violence tonight. I could use my gun
on him. Instead, I grab my brother with my left hand and hit
him with my right. The chador burns next to us, swallowing
the fire in itself.

After one punch, I leave my brother in the courtyard. I
bleed geography out of my nose: Ecuador, Albania, Nairobi.
All the places we can still go, once I find you.

26

The cypress tree in front of your childhood home has grown enough to block most of the front door. From the street we could always see your aunt sitting in her chair in the dark. Somehow her silhouette was deeper than the rest of the room, even if the room was pitch-black. And she sat at an angle so she could see all that went on outside, the world that rarely brought her any joy. With the growth of the tree, she's adjusted her seat in the house.

From where I stand in the front yard, I can tell she's moved over several inches to keep as much of the view as possible.

Since your father wasn't her blood relative, she wore a scarf at all times around the house. And when she cut her hair, she hid it in a canister of Ahmad Shah tea, the one with the duck on the label.

"And once a month," you said, "she digs a hole in the backyard to bury her hair." So devout, she probably didn't even want the sun to see. "She folds a handful into a braid, ties the end with a ribbon, then cuts off the whole thing."

We tried digging out a few of the Ahmad Shah tea canisters in the yard, one of many mounds lining the edges. We gave up after shoveling a dozen holes. Her hair out of solidarity must have curled into rocks. I pass by those holes someone has since covered on my way to our hiding place.

Your aunt never made you sleep in the basement, but we had fun pretending we were banished under the house. A beehive hangs on the hinges of the wooden-plank entrance. I try to wade my way through the darkness as gently as possible even though most of the bees have taken cover in their hive for the night. We used to joke that with the proper hole through the basement ceiling, the bees could go upward into the house to attack your aunt so it'd be yours, not hers.

I head toward your desk under the house. I light the path with my phone. The drawers are empty, not because you've erased the memories, but because you never held on to papers like I did, bookmarks and paper clips that remind me of essays on Althusser, verse by Attar of Nishapur, and torn-out screenplay pages from *Criss Cross* you made me read. After each school year ended, you'd throw all ephemera away. There is no proof leading you to me.

Your aunt's nightingales go quiet when I knock on the front door. Their cages swing when I let myself in. Each has a thick lace cover.

"Who's there?" your aunt asks from the dark. I stand in the light that comes from the street. She's bothered when she realizes it's just me. "You look like a riddle that's half-finished."

I pull my sleeves down and hide my arm hair that I swear feels softer now.

"You know where Zal is?"

She grins. "You're always asking the same question. Always chasing him. Funny, I've never seen him do the same for you."

"Funny," I say. "I've never heard anyone ask for you."

"She was in love once," you explained. She was engaged until a crow flew directly into her face with its beak aimed at her pupil.

Your aunt gestures to the tea set next to her. "Do you still read fortunes?"

"Why? Do you want me to tell yours?"

"There's no need. There's only one way for this life to go. Though I'm sure you see all kinds of catastrophes." Your aunt smiles. "Grieving becomes you, my dear."

"Am I in mourning?" Does she know where you are now?

"You should be."

Her languid way of speaking reminds me of the time you said, "Loving you is tossing blood into an oblivion."

I leave your aunt alone again. From outside I hear the exaggerated sounds of her scissors, cutting her braid clean off. If ever I am to visit this house again, I know the cypress tree will grow big enough to eclipse the full front door. She might prefer it that way.

The Haft-Hoze fountains pause—all seven—until I reach the apartment you share with your wife. The city stops, even

161

the jays usually known for their lyrical flight. I pass a mirror headboard leaning against a garbage bin. The rectangle of glass is attached to three-foot posts. The wood is ready to buckle from the weight of the glass, perhaps after years of witnessing bedroom conversations that shouldn't be repeated. When I reach your door, time returns. A quick start. The fountains burst a few extra feet until the water reaches an equilibrium, time as it is, not as I want it to be.

It was with animosity that I bought nightingales for you, identical to the ones your aunt keeps. The birds chirp when I approach your apartment on the fifth floor. They're onto me.

27

Our last fuck was our most vicious. I spoke about killing your wife. You covered my mouth when I settled on the easiest plan, even though I couldn't remember which of your films it came from. A torn necklace in the tub. We could make it look like she slipped and hit her head. Or feed her sleeping pills in the bath, so long as she slumped underneath. Add in some empty gin bottles and an inquest would be less likely. You covered my mouth not because you wanted me to shut up. You started fucking me faster.

I sometimes think your marriage was the result of an argument we had. You left, you came back, and you said that you were engaged. "She's a nice woman, really. The kind of person I should probably end up with."

I couldn't stomach picturing you with anyone else. To keep me safe, my mind interceded. I felt nothing. Detachment became my ace. My bones gave up their corners in my delirium.

You fed me for the day, as you'd done during a more worrisome fever. I blankly watched the spoon you used to scoop my chin when soup spilled from my mouth. You were surprised by my surprise, that I didn't respond by yelling or throwing a fit. You set down the bowl of barley soup and kissed me as if that was enough to undo the decision to wed someone other than me.

"I look forward to meeting her," I said once I decided to speak again.

I wondered if we would stop fucking.

We didn't. That night I whispered things that might sound dull now, but at the time hurried your climax: Does she do this with you too? Does she let you put it in there? Does she smile, does she whimper, does she get off when you weep?

You responded with the heaviest load that felt like a fist punching my forehead. I laughed. "You're gonna give me a black eye."

"The bitch," I thought when I first met Mahtob. It was a shock to be introduced to her, a meeting you planned out of spite. She had wealth. I could tell by the Dior logo on her scarf, bag, and shoes, all a similar faint pink.

"I'm glad to meet someone who knew this rascal when he was a kid." She tousled your hair from across the table.

"We don't deserve this much joy," you said pointedly. You held up her ring finger.

"Considering all he's been through," she said. "Just him and his aunt now. He deserves a proportionate amount of bliss. I bet he was always looking for that special woman to grow old and die with."

I wanted her to grow old and die right then.

After shaking her hand, the limpest handshake I hope ever to experience, I looked down at my pathetic shirt, thin to keep your eyes fixated on my neck where your hand always landed at the end of intimacy. It was a poor attempt at seduction. I thought of the bone that doesn't exist after death. I fixated on your crotch.

Mahtob leaned across the table diagonally toward me. "Is it true your father was a bigamist?" For some reason, she immediately tried for humiliation.

I felt myself being forgotten, a secret you'd never speak of again. I wanted to balance the scales because you thought you were spurning me. I caught you looking down my neck, at my clavicle and chest. It wasn't over between us.

Mahtob pouted because we hadn't gotten our water glasses yet.

"The service here leaves much to be desired." She was probably used to the hotels where men with towels over their arms choreographed pleasantries. You twitched when I put my hand in your pant pocket. She didn't notice. "Is it all buffet style?" Mahtob asked, staring behind her.

Oblivious woman. She was confused by the lunch special, platters of kabob and fresh mint. While she faced the kitchen to grab someone's attention, I spit a thick quick drip onto your pants, right at the crotch. As brazen as ever. It only made the bulge grow. I know how to let a wad dangle from my tongue because you realized I never learned how to properly spit loogies, so we practiced by shooting down snails. Eventually I got the hang of it, making it a party trick I used on your dick.

I didn't feel bad for grabbing your cock under the restaurant table. It was your fault for sitting next to me and across from your wife. The thought of you in bed telling her my secrets was enough to make me loosen your belt. She fumbled with the menu and almost dropped it. I'd have liked to see her expression as I jostled your dick through your pocket. It was mine in a way it could never be hers. It owed its pleasure to me. You couldn't make a fuss about me stroking your dick without admitting I had done it before.

"Really," she pouted. "I'll die of dehydration."

You nodded. "They should be here soon." It was delightful watching you try to keep your voice even while I rubbed the tip of your cock with my thumb. You dropped your napkin on your lap and stood up using a menu to cover your hard-on, excusing yourself to complain about the table service. Some precum seeped through your pocket onto my thumb. I licked my fingers in a way I'm sure disgusted Mahtob. Your precum only whetted my appetite for what you did hours later down my throat. Yes. I still had power over you.

28

Your wife opens the door to your shared apartment.

"I've been waiting for you." She always reverts to her disgusting smile. It's a ploy. She has more teeth than mouth.

Mahtob scratches the aluminum foil under her scarf, itchy from a new dollop of bleach. She looks out the window and points at a tree as if she's motioning to someone. Under her veil, I see her dressing gown, one you bought for her to wear. Obligation, of course. Not love.

"Have you seen Zal?" I ask her. Straight to the point.

Mahtob returns to tweezing her eyebrows like I'm not there. With her right pinky, she measures the space between the beginning of her nose and each eyebrow to make sure they are even. They never will be. With an exhale, she tugs a few ends from the underside of her brow. Momentarily I wonder how much her eyelashes will grow after death.

"How's your mother?" she asks with an appropriate amount of malice.

"Still a little lost."

"Must run in the family. You know your share of sins."

"Coming from you, it's sort of a compliment." A fake smile from us both.

The phone rings. She answers it immediately as if the ringing alone will give away her secrets. She lowers her voice. I can tell she's talking to a man by the tone. She hides in the kitchen. When she leaves the room, I measure the space between my nose and either eyebrow. I picture myself playing her part. Bleaching my hair. Tweezing my brows. Plumping my lips with red.

She circles me after hanging up. "My poor mother. Terribly sick."

"Have you seen Zal?" I ask again.

"Is he missing?"

She closes a window for discretion, even though her bleach fumes burn our eyes. "I've always wanted to live alone. I never had the opportunity. Went from living with my family to living with Zal."

"I'm sure you indulge in pleasure when he's out of town."

She looks at me. No jokes. No animosity. "I wish there was a wading pool. I wish I had time to consider who I really wanted to spend my life with. You're luckier in that respect. There are certain parts of your life you can choose with discretion. Because you're a man. There are certain places you can go, and there's less of a deadline to decide what you want from life."

She gestures to three packed bags by the front door. Three suitcases, each with matching silver locks. On an end table, I spot a dirty glass, gray from old skin. Perhaps your wife collects still lifes of you with others, just like me. The lip marks align with mine. Perhaps I'm the still life here, the Flemish flies on peonies reminding us both of death. Or the dirty dish is a dirty dish. After all, your wife's not that deep.

"I don't want to be married to Zal anymore. That's the truth. I need you to get rid of someone for me. And I'll leave you two alone. I'll even tell you where Zal is. Win-win."

"You're not the only threat."

"Whatever do you mean? You think there's this brilliant network out to get you? No. Just me."

"Who took the photos?"

"The photographer? He's the man I want to leave with."

"Why are you telling me all of this?"

"There's no harm. You can't reveal my secrets without letting out your own. I wanted those photos of you because I needed proof. Not just words. Actions. Fluids." Her tone shifts. "I won't be stuck like my mother was. Not because of that awful man. When he's gone, Zal and I will have five million to split easily. Otherwise, my father will outlive us all. He has a wide definition of degenerates."

Mahtob runs her fingers down her throat. We share a desperation that's unavoidable: We know that we are both aging, that the more we wait, the less time we'll have with the wicked men we love. It isn't her words that soften me, but that gesture, hand on neck, calculating how long before gravity knocks down her skin another half inch.

"Don't you have enough money?"

"It's nothing compared to what he'll leave behind. You've never even met my father, so you won't have to worry about a thing. Consider it. You won't be able to run away safely unless we have an understanding. You can escape with Zal, but I can easily interrupt. Lucky for you, we each have someone new."

She senses my hesitation.

"You know where he is?"

"A favor for me. A favor for you."

"I need some time."

"No use overthinking. My father's leaving for Frankfurt again." She plops down a newspaper. "I saw this and thought of you."

To clinch the deal, she motions to an article about the public hanging. The citron grove.

"Take a good look," she says. "The family business. My father's the one grinning right next to the citron tree." His mustache is half-white, half-black. Of all people, I shouldn't be surprised by the cruelty of kin. "It's an easy decision, no? A life for a life. His for yours."

"You say it like it's nothing."

"My father has made it easier for us than he knows. He keeps his car for sentimental reasons. Supposedly had Persepolis stone ground into the silver paint. More than anything, he's hooked on the luxuries of his car. Simple features they've advanced with newer models. But he likes what he likes, his customization. The seats lower, the mirrors tilt, the seat belt tightens. Simple. Adjusts for whoever unlocks the car. Even me." She holds out an extra key fob for her father's vehicle. Just two simple buttons. Unlock and lock. "He can be so stubborn. Never cared for recalls, even if there are hazards."

"How will this help?"

"Poor thing. The seat belt will be good and taut. The mechanism even rolls the strap back behind the seat just for me. Makes me feel safe, but might lock him in place so he can't move. Use my key to unlock the car while he's driving. Even if you're next to the car. A fault. The seat belt will tighten to my preset and won't unbuckle until the car is off. He can swing the door open, but won't be able to get out."

"Hardly sounds like enough of a plan."

"A seat belt. And his tea. That's our recipe."

"Tea?"

"He drinks morphine with his. Just a touch. Carries around his own tea kettle. Takes the edge off long drives. That, and auto drive."

"And you're sure?" I ask. "You sure you want him gone?"

She nods. "Some blasphemies won't be forgiven."

She must have been dealt a deck of suicide kings. Mahtob leaves the room to turn on the faucet of her bathtub. Her phone rings while she unwraps the foil from her hair. I answer before it lets out more than one chirp.

"Where?" I blurt in a whisper over the phone.

He pauses for a few seconds, whomever it is. He didn't expect anyone to answer so quickly. "Your pick."

"Azar hotel. 7:43 A.M. Tomorrow." I hang up.

Mahtob returns to the room. I look at her expression to see if she's picked up on anything. With the gun in my pocket, it'd be easy to get it all over with right now. But killing her wouldn't guarantee the inheritance. Not yet. I'm tempted by the thought of getting rid of anyone who could discuss how well you use your dick.

I pause before I go. "Do you ever think it might be easier elsewhere? A different country, perhaps? A decade or so from now?"

She doesn't bat an eye. "Aziz, everyone has a trap with a different name." Mahtob spots my necklaces of blue beads. She toys with them. "You always were the one I thought he'd end up with anyway. When I met you. I could tell."

"I doubt it."

"A wife knows her rival."

29

The best rendezvous times are not fully rounded hours, especially if you are meeting someone in secret. An odd time makes it feel more impromptu. 6:24, 11:17, 7:43.

I imagine your wife's lover has a brilliant poker face. He must be a mirror image of me trying to find ways to kill off her husband. Maybe he succeeded this time and they are rid of you. You have no parents to look for you. And your aunt would hardly care. All Mahtob and her lover would have to do is hide a few of your belongings and say you were elsewhere waiting for me. But she needs this favor first.

It has to be him in the lobby. I can tell. Mahtob has settled for someone who could pass as you. He arrives as planned at 7:43 A.M., with his sleeves stained with ash. He checks his watch three times.

The hotel kitchen staff hands me a teacup with a carafe of coffee.

"For him," the server says. He nods to the patio where Mahtob's lover slumps at a table.

He sits staring at a plate of apples dotted with bruises. He's moved the floral centerpiece to the floor, probably to clear the table of sentimentality. The dahlias droop beside his dress socks. He's shirt sleeves are rolled up, and his tie with a diagonal stripe is loosened. He's already over the day. Seated next to him, his overcoat. Cloves perfume the table, like the empty elevator in the hotel, like the lobby of my apartment.

I want to ask him if photographing us gave him a rise. "You've been following me," I say. At the cemetery, in the bazaar. I assume he's the one who killed the cat.

"Maybe."

"To see how the other half lives?"

He swirls the remaining coffee at the bottom of his glass.

"Sit," he says without looking.

"I can't."

He grabs my hand. "Please."

I hear the frustration in his voice because he expected her, not me.

"You have a name?"

He hesitates, but realizes it's the quickest way to get me to join him. "Kaveh."

I sit. I figure he's some sort of draftsman based on the specialty mechanical pencils in his shirt pocket. He's orderly, but tired. The back of his neck is red from a self-trim to keep the nape tidy. Stress lines ruin his otherwise handsome face. He's not some Rostam lothario, just a jilted architect whose life made a severe detour.

I pour him more coffee once he downs his cup. He lights a clove cigarette, but doesn't smoke any of it. I can picture

Mahtob telling him every detail in your bedroom, letting him in on her secrets: her dark roots, her old nose, her husband's infidelity.

"I wondered what you looked like up close," I say.

"Am I everything you imagined?"

"Yes. Devastating." He flips a matchbook between his fingers. "How'd you two meet?"

"At the orchard. A simple, stupid tour."

He pulls out a bottle of children's aspirin. The pills are pastel pink to make them less daunting for kids. Kaveh pops one.

"Want something stronger?" I ask.

"Can't handle more. Makes me sick."

Kaveh looks at the highest floor of the hotel. I know that stare. He calculates the number of somersaults a body would make before it tongues the earth.

"You know how to get to the family orchard?" I ask.

He pulls out a map that's not only folded, but rolled from impatience.

"Roughly."

I spread out the paper and take a look at the route to the citron groves. There is a stop that's familiar to me on the way. A good enough lookout point.

"You going to help me?" I ask him.

Kaveh looks down at his hand, at stains he's since washed.

"Vice makes you shrink," he says. "My mother always told me so. I still think about it sometimes." He places his

175

hand on the table and pulls out a fountain pen. Very gently, he traces around his fingers. With his fork he measures the length. "Yup," he sighs. "It really does make you shrink."

"If I can escape with Zal, you can escape with her."

He considers it for a moment and nods once.

30

Kaveh and I walk around the Shahrak in Ghazali, the partially abandoned outdoor movie set made to look centuries old. They film period pieces and soap operas here. It's free to enter, and there are no attendants. We stand on the periphery of the movie set and look out onto the road. The citron orchard is seven miles away. We keep watch for Mahtob's father, his car.

To pass the time, we wind through a dirt road with several abandoned carriages. There's grime under each one from mud splatter. Shopwindows with hand-painted fruit on the panes signal the market. Kaveh stops at a storefront.

"I followed Mahtob here once. It's where she meets all her men."

In a doorway, a dervish costume hangs with crescent sequins down the sides, probably from a film scheduled to shoot later in the day. Kaveh carries his coat over his arm more often than he wears it. He looks so much like you.

We've kissed on this film set before during a day trip. You said, "Maybe if we stow away in old Persia, then we can carve a riddle in which we could live. If we tuck in this corner, behind this cart, then we can stay here hidden in time until two other lovers come to take our place."

"Talk is a waste of life."

"This is my life," you said.

Some days it sounded romantic, and some days it just sounded sad. That day, it was the latter. A security guard told us it was time to leave, so we left. There were no portals, but I wanted my damnedest to argue with time. Other lovers might not count the hours in blinks and exhales like we do.

"We're lucky to be unlucky," you joked. It was an attempt to get the melancholy off my chin, like any sweet that was once indulged. It was another of those things that shifted meaning based on when you said it, depending on how orange the sunset was, and if that day out of ache I wished us both dead.

They're shooting a film in the ghost town. Kaveh watches.

"We need more blood," the director says.

The crew scrambles in a swell of activity. Three people dig through bags. A woman on a walkie calls around for more. An actor lies face down on the pavement waiting for extra blood to be poured over his neck while interns mix together juice and coloring.

"No, no, no." The director isn't amused with this batch. "We need more blood. Real blood." Whatever that means.

Kaveh burns and releases matches, clove-scented like his cigarettes.

"You should be careful with those," I say.

"There are worse dangers to my health."

"You leave your stink wherever you go."

"Maybe it's intentional."

"Whose blood was it? At the apartment."

"I hurt myself. You'll be happy to know your lobby is easy to break into, but not your front door."

Maybe for an amateur, which I don't believe he is. Any compassion I have turns sexual with men. Easily his head could fall on my chest. In profile especially, his cheekbones would fit with no edges.

"You mind?" a man asks from a dark pathway between two building facades. "Your smoke is lousing up the picture quality."

Kaveh puts the matches away. I peek into the darkness that envelopes the man. There's a whole setup of monitors and extension cords overloading one of the few circuits onsite. An editor pieces together footage on a laptop, shots recorded that day. A flat-screen TV plays back live camera footage from the set, where the director continues to beg for more and more blood. Off to the side, hidden partially under a tablecloth, a small projector puffs out some footage on the wall. It's the size of a sheet of paper, just some sample of whatever film stock they're testing. The flicker. The talk of blood. The buzz from the nine extension cords overloading one plug. It all makes me think of you.

I remember when we stood at a stairwell and tried to make ourselves fall because of some movie we'd watched. A 16mm print survived the fires the zealots burned after the revolution. But a few films bobbed out decades later. A neighbor found canisters in the former red-light district. I happened to be in my dad's way when he ran to grab an empty paint can he used to hold his opium.

"Bring your friend," he said instead of pushing me aside. It beat tossing dead fish at each other from the pet store's garbage.

We sat in a back room and watched a film that had deteriorated into acid pink. The other men lost interest, because they expected to see something they remembered from youth, *Bonnie and Clyde* or *Psycho*. They left. When the first reel ended, we tried our best to switch it ourselves.

"Fine," the projectionist said when he caught us. "But only so you can watch the ending."

He quickly fed the spool into the projector and played it at double speed while he packed up to play backgammon with the others. At least we got to see Gene Tierney throw herself down stairs, a moment I recreated and as a result chipped a tooth.

"Blood. More blood," the director continues to bark on the screen with the live feed of the film shoot.

Let that be my refrain. Blood. More blood.

I hold my breath for seven seconds, then exhale very slowly. I have on your pants. The blood stains are faint now, and the heat from pushing against Omid's crotch is gone. I have them on to keep me close to you. The edges of the belt loops rub my wrists until they itch, and the pockets easily fit the gun.

"Everything okay?" Kaveh asks. I've dropped my guard against my better judgment. Smaller signs of greater panic are showing. More blood. Cut and cut and cut. Before I can answer, Kaveh pulls me close to his body so I don't get hit by a worker swinging a ladder over his shoulder.

"Watch it!" Kaveh yells on my behalf.

"Buddy, if you're gonna crowd our workspace, you assume the liabilities."

We pause a moment longer than most people would after being accidentally pulled together.

"You have any idea where Zal is?" I ask.

"Not yet."

"Mahtob was waiting for you yesterday. Her bags were packed."

"Was she?" He smiles. "Maybe she was making a break for it, leaving us both behind."

"Maybe."

Kaveh sighs. "I can't wait for it to even out, the all-nighter that's gone on for months. I'll be able to roll down my sleeves, put on my coat, and tighten my tie. Go home. Sleep with my beloved without any more obstacles."

"You're almost there. Almost in the second act of your sordid affair."

"I hope. Does Zal have any other family? Do you know that much?"

"I know almost everything about him."

In the distance, a car speeds down the highway. Silver with gold rims. On its way to the citron orchard.

Kaveh stares at the car. "Almost is enough to lose yourself in."

31

The road to the orchard is a straight shot most of the way. The highway doesn't change directions. However, a small space on the eastern side of the street goes from hairline crack to full-on canyon. This geological form is my gift. The cliff is not massive, but deep enough to bless us with a wreck. There is one sharp turn before the fruit trees. A tour bus headed to the orchard unloads passengers so they can offer the driver some guidance.

Cypresses mark the entrance of the grove. The place is surrounded by narcoleptic cats that circle themselves before dropping down to sleep. I hardly seem out of place, since there are enthusiastic crowds wandering the site. After leaving their bus, tourists take pictures of themselves holding whatever fruit they can reach. Others set their phones on self-timer and hurry to pose for photos.

I recognize Mahtob's father because of his mustache: half-white and half-black. He walks around with a tiny glass of tea. It would be easy to poison considering how often he refills it. On top of his silver monstrosity of a car, he places a handkerchief. He stirs a tiny serving of morphine into a tea-pot with a comically long spout. The unlabeled bottle goes in and out of his coat pocket. As he walks around to survey the field, he continues to carry his small tea glass for a few sips.

With one hand, he flips open a pocketknife and stabs into a citron. Just by smelling it, he can tell everything that's wrong with the crop. "Too much alkalinity in the water." He doesn't close the blade before sticking it back in his pocket.

A drowsy cat follows me. It circles around my left foot before plopping down. I look closer and realize it isn't asleep. They've been poisoned. A worker clobbers his way through the trees and tosses the dead cats over his shoulder so he can get rid of their bodies. When he's closer, four trees away, I try to hide by picking citrons from a branch. The worker stops to wipe his forehead. Instead of the bandanna around his neck, he accidentally grabs a cat by the tail, causing the mostly dead thing to kick.

I might as well ask him a question in the privacy of the trees.

"Do you know who reported the man who was killed?"

"You another journalist?" he asks after turning his head to spit. "There's nothing new about the hanging that you haven't read elsewhere."

"Which tree was it?"

He welcomes the opportunity to pause his task. "One farther east."

An unplanned question comes to mind. "After he died, did they cut down the branch or just the rope?"

"Branch? For the weight of a full body, they couldn't just use one branch. Had to climb and tie six of 'em together to support the weight. I slid down the rope myself as a test, just to make sure it wouldn't snap. We had to climb up with a machete to hack away at the tree after he died. That's how you can tell which it was. On the periphery. In view of the packing house. With a giant bald spot gashed out."

A loud yell tears through the groves. A pipe has burst. Workers gather around the gush of water. Some in their haste grab buckets, while others run far to twist pipes and stop the outpour, higher than the tallest cypresses. Mahtob's father grabs the collar of a woman, a fruit picker in from the field.

"Do something!" he yells.

I feel my own collar tighten.

His brash gesture loosens the woman's veil. In panic she pulls back. She double knots her scarf with one hand while handing trash can lids to men to stop the spout. It's futile, since no amount of pots, pans, or lids will do a thing to calm the water, a burst that pushes up and away, that catapults men who try to snuff it with their weight. A moat deepens around the pipe.

It's the perfect time to tamper with his tea like we have planned. A subtle anticlimax of a death, hopefully into a canyon on his drive away. I sneak toward the silver car. I hide behind the trunk and make my way to the driver's side. The kettle lid makes no noise when I lift it, or when I replace it. Four additional capfuls. Plenty without adding bitterness to his drink.

Kaveh joins me after parking our getaway car.

"All set?" he asks.

"More than enough morphine. He'll fall asleep behind the wheel."

I can tell Kaveh is wondering how his life fumbled to bring him vices he thinks make his neck thinner and his knees regress. It's either for being an adulterer or for plotting with someone like me. He steps away from a citron tree and imagines himself from a month ago. He nods as if the comparison is clear. We're both shrinking. He adjusts his belt since the buckle has swiveled all the way to the side.

A new thought crosses his mind. "What if he just pulls his foot off the gas when he falls asleep?" An idea comes to him. "I'll be back."

He leaves me between trees, one of them pale at the bark. The side is gashed out completely, and molasses drips more dramatically than blood.

Kaveh returns. It's clear he's inching toward the end of his nerves. His rage is more impressive than his gentleness. It makes him candid. I savor being a passenger to someone else's undoing.

"We're in this together," he says. There's something erotic about it. "If the old man steps on the gas all the way, it'll stick. We just need to make sure he presses it down completely."

"How?"

"We might need to get in the car with him." He puts his hand on my shoulder. "You think you can do it?"

"Me?"

"You have to. You're smaller. You're less conspicuous than me."

32

While waiting inside the old man's luxury car, I remember Panj's prompt from the party. Think of a first anything to kill time.

We were sixteen. Smells in your car: ass, halva, cigarettes. The third day of the third week of the new year. I left school after an argument. Before we had a chance to reconcile, my dad forced me to go to Qamsar as a punishment for what he suspected was growing between us.

"You'll have time." My dad repeated over and over again on the drive. The phrase was meant for us both. I'd have time in my grandmother's village to recover from my sins, and he'd have time to decide on a more violent outcome if I didn't.

You drove for hours to see me. You were shocked when you saw my face, the scars I pretended were from thorns. The other workers were always very kind. They wondered why I wept so much. They thought I was malnourished, so they brought me sweet milk in glass jars.

"Drink up, my child. It'll be okay."

I drank every ounce, even though I didn't need to.

You showed up in your old car painted with a stripe and took me away. We found an abandoned house with no doors and no windows and no doorframes and no windowframes. The mud walls were peeling from expanding and contracting in heat. We barely made it past the front entrance before you dropped my pants and started to fuck me. Our first time, if I am to pick.

You fucked me before we even kissed that day. I worried if I was clean enough to be penetrated, but you didn't care. And I didn't mind either, even though I knew I was being torn. To be polite we wiped our cum off the floor and into the wall. I joked that because of you, I'd shit pearls for weeks. The rest of humanity may celebrate Shabeh-Yalda, the winter solstice, as the longest night of the year. To me that night in the mud house will always be the longest of any eternity. Afterward, we made planets by connecting thorn wounds on my arms.

Mahtob was right. All the luxuries of the old man's car will work against him. The windows are tinted so dark, he can't tell I'm huddled on the floor behind his leather seat. It adjusts before he even enters the car. I'm crammed in place. His tall armrest is a sort of partition. I don't need to hunch as much as I do, but better to be safe.

The old man buckles in and rolls down his window.

"We'll test the alkaline level again in a month," he says out the window to a worker. "When I'm back from Frankfurt." He turns on the ignition.

"You look tired," his employee tells him. "You okay?"

"Of course. I just didn't expect so much pipe damage before I retired."

I'm glad for the moment. I'm glad someone else witnesses what could later be interpreted as distress.

"You sure you don't want me to drive you?"

The old man laughs. "And what'll I do? Sleep in the back?"

God no.

"Just a suggestion."

Mahtob's father starts to drive away. He reaches for his tea, but gives up after missing the cup holder twice. He turns on his radio. It's all static. He looks at himself in the mirror, dries his mustache with his collar. There's a coat in his back seat, some cheap fur knockoff. It's bunched next to me.

He reaches for the glass again and finds it. He finally takes a sip, then downs the whole thing like a shot and doesn't flinch from the taste. He grows drowsy near the cypress tree entrance. The car slows down. I peek. His head sways from side to side. The way he fusses around in the glove compartment, it's obvious the car is now on auto. It's a straight shot for several miles, with the most ready danger to our left: a canyon deep enough for his death. The old man reaches for his teapot to pour himself more tea. Must like the extra morphine. I dig deep in my pocket for Mahtob's key. Left button. I press unlock. She was right. The driver's seat adjusts. Surprised, the old man drops the kettle on his lap.

"Goddamn." With one window down and another open a tiny crack, a howl pierces through the car.

His seat belt tightens back. I help by lodging the strap behind the headrest to make it especially tight. He's slow to react. His hands dart upward to find some way to set himself free. From the back seat, I hold on to his forearms when he tenses up. The car continues driving itself forward. He's too panicked about suffocating to reach for the button that would stop the cruise control mechanism. Instead, he's fixated on choking, and the hands of a stranger holding his wrists back. I whisper in his ear.

"You are fine. Just close your eyes."

He closes his eyes, not to accept his fate, but to see if the nightmare will end with just that blink. Nope.

"It'll be fine," I whisper. "It's almost over."

I lull him. The niceness of my greeting catches him off guard. I meet him in the hallucination his mind already builds. He quiets down.

Let him be the stand-in. It's the only way I can go through with it. I tell myself this over and over again. Let him stand in for the vile men who deserve their own violence.

For a brief moment of lucidity, Mahtob's father breaks free from my hands and reaches for the latch to adjust his seat. Can't take off the belt, but can at least adjust the seat incline. Release. The seat falls back and pummels into me. The belt tightens around his neck. In franticness, he charges the seat forward with his full weight, smashes his chest into the steering wheel. The teapot on his lap pivots. He pulls back, then pushes his chest upright again. The tea spout points toward him. In that final lunge forward, he smashes himself into something with such force, a single tight strand of blood gushes outward onto the front window. The knife in his pocket. I swear, the puncture squeals. His blood pours into the teapot through the spout. He collapses backward from damage and delirium, no more movement except a few nerves pinching themselves in shock.

The car continues steadily. From the back seat, I check the speedometer. Not faster than thirty miles an hour. Almost makes me laugh, the bloodshed the outside world can't yet see. Forward on a straight line. His foot weighs down the gas pedal. Not too fast yet. Thirty-five, forty. Perfect.

I try to open my door, back seat behind the driver. It doesn't budge. I crawl over to the other side. Doesn't budge either. I press lock and unlock on the key fob, still down deep in my pocket. Mechanical sounds. No movement since the seat is already positioned in Mahtob's preset. The doors, however, stay locked. I crawl over the armrest to the passenger's side. I pull the door handle. No luck. A quirk she lied about on purpose. The doors don't unlock if the car is running. She wants to make sure he dies, that I die too. That bitch.

She believed what she said: Some blasphemies won't be forgiven.

I can escape only if I do so out the driver-side window. I grab the coat from the back seat, the cheap fake with three-inch-long fur.

Keep me safe, I tell the fox.

I climb on the old man's lap. It's an unexpected intimacy being so close to him. Here is the man. It's not important if he was one of the killers or a sadistic bystander. He meets me in the hallucination my mind already builds. Let him be the stand-in, because even if I undergo the change, even if I abide by the law and have my paperwork adjusted, the madness of the simpleminded could be enough for murder.

I reach outside the window and grab the handle. His door opens. I push it wide. I know how to jump and tuck my arms. Because the car is going faster than I hoped, I try to take his foot off the gas. It's stuck. Really stuck. I have no choice but to jump. My coat soaks in some of his blood. The blade dislodges from his chest. Blood, morphine, and bergamot drip onto his dress socks. Sixty-five, seventy. Faster. There are no other cars around. So I do it. I jump. Through the howl of the window. I flop outward with my arms tucked, my head tucked too.

I roll. I swear, something guides me. Something cradles me. I glide. It could be the coat. The fur tears to pieces people will confuse for roadkill. But a hand delivers me down softly onto earth, a tumble of movement. Once I stop rolling, once it's safe for me to extend my head and stretch out my arms, I start to heave. Not because of what I've done, his blood soaked on my hem. I was able to jump out of the car and not break my neck. That shocks me. Whatever held me, whatever caught me delivered me with damage only to the coat. But I'm not grateful for this miracle, because it didn't come to my life soon enough.

I tighten what's left of the coat around me. Kaveh pulls up several minutes later.

"Hurry," he says. I hop in. "I couldn't keep up. Not without drawing attention."

In front of us, the old man's car drives forward where it would have ordinarily pivoted. The sharp turn. The silver car tips over the edge, deepens the canyon when he finally collides with the earth. Like tracing the lacerations on my mother's head, I feel every bit of pain myself. Sitting in the center of a fire I built for another man. Smoke bobs up from the wreck.

Kaveh is surprised I'm not hurt. "You sure you didn't hit your head?"

"I'm sure."

He pulls his seat closer to the steering wheel. We say nothing, but both wonder if he really did shrink an inch or two.

"We'll have to get rid of the coat," he says.

He cares about me for some reason, doesn't want to leave me with any evidence. Maybe he didn't expect me to go through with it. Maybe he didn't expect me to survive. But me being there, scratched up, rouged with another man's blood, does something to him. Makes him perk up. Makes him linger when he looks at me the way only certain men do. Nothing divine, just luck. Rarely good. Often bad. Always there.

33

Kaveh paces in our Sodom just to keep watch over me for a little longer. Sighing could be his catchphrase. Much like I regret loving a man, maybe he regrets loving a married woman.

"You sure you don't feel dizzy?" He's still worried I have a concussion.

"It wouldn't be the worst thing."

He sits down on the couch. I can't help but notice a leaf caught on his lap to the left of his zipper. His legs are so wide-open, I want to sit down on the floor next to his knees and rub one before letting my hand linger. I could be his footstool. My adrenaline gets me hard.

I serve Kaveh a drink. After he downs his scotch, I take the glass and set it on the table. He puts his hands together and breathes into them even though it isn't cold. He places a clove cigarette in the corner of his mouth.

"Were you home when Zal came in with that young man?"

"I was probably dreaming. Blame the pills."

He stands to take matches out of his coat pocket. We face each other. He lights one and lets it burn down to his fingers. By the time the fire gets too close to his middle fingernail, I get on my knees and blow it out. He likes it. He burns another one. Because he likes it, I let it burn even further. This time I don't blow it out. He shakes to snuff the flame. I stand and lean in close. Cloves. With the heat of his crotch, my pubes crinkle. Against his misgivings, he leans in to kiss me as if murder is a sort of aphrodisiac. He stops. Perhaps he kissed her last and doesn't want to interrupt the taste. He pulls back.

"Meet me one more time," Kaveh says.

"I can't."

Men are drawn to me, I know it, because I ache.

"Please." With me, a different taboo opens its trap for him.

"We'd look ridiculous in Isfahan." There, people dance in slow motion to keep from drawing attention, and the elderly maids clear the tablecloths before couples are done eating.

"We can stay at a different hotel. Different from where you go with him."

"But the labyrinthine one is best." The third day of the third week of the new year.

He grabs my shoulders. Always the same gesture. Here, look at me. A poor actor's trick. As soon as our lips touch, Kaveh snaps me around. A quick, almost athletic move jolts me into knowing that even though I tempted a kiss, he's in control. But I use my tongue well. Soon I take power back. I give myself a goodbye kiss through him. I become him for a moment and the kiss comes backward to me. Is that how I do it? Henceforth let me remember to use more teeth. I fall into the wide grimace of his mouth knowing we won't meet again.

34

In our room in my uncle's hotel, I do my best to get rid of our evidence. Any drug I have hidden there becomes something to sink into the toilet. The pipes will wobble from all the acid they take. I pack the sleeping pills. I'll need help for the various countdowns. To surgeries, to reunions.

I remake the bed to buy a few more minutes in our hideaway. Before exiting, I open the sliding door to the balcony all the way, so my body heat can be licked cold again. Soon my uncle will install stoppers to keep the sliding doors from opening completely. Too many people must contemplate jumping after overthinking what comes next. Others will inhabit the rooms in which we've fucked, and suck the street air we swallowed in kisses, but no one will see the gestures that meant so much to us on weightier days. We are smoke from a candle that will never exist again.

I head to the apartment you share with Mahtob to tell her the task is complete. I enter the building from the back to be safe. Strips of the interior carpeting are rolled out front. A sacrilege if they were pulled from your apartment where we slept, laid, talked, fucked a few times when she was out of town. The rolls are heavy with flies, probably sniffing around every bodily fluid we had to offer. I wait until there are no sounds in the hallway before climbing up. I knock softly. Mahtob doesn't answer.

Outside the door of the apartment, I swear I hear a conversation. Her and a man. Then just a man's voice.

Yours? I can't tell. The murmur is enough. And one at a time, metallic sounds echo. Birdcages. The nightingales are frantic. They leap around and pound their wings and heads and beaks against the sides of the cages. But like petals tossed off a flower, eventually there are less and less. From the open window leading to the fire escape of the building, I hear the birds thrown out. Someone coughs on the balcony. I see the shoulders of someone who jumps to the fire escape and makes a break for it. I take a look when he is at least two flights down. At the window a few of the remaining nightingales circle. They don't go any farther than several feet. They obscure my sight as the body dives into the night, down to join the abyss of the street.

I return to her front door. I ring the bell one more time. No response. No movement. From a neighbor's apartment, a radio plays a violin sonata over and over again. It takes me a beat to work up the nerve to go inside. I have enough octagonal pills left, if it comes down to it. Easy to slip her into a tub to go to sleep. Easy to finish with pearl bullets, if need be, if she defies our plan. The front door is unlocked. Fools. I go inside.

"Anyone here?" I ask. "Mahtob?" Named after moonlight, I sense she'd be in plain view. But even though there is warmth in the room from the reverb of an ended conversation, no one responds.

In the bathroom, the tub is overflowing. At this hour, the water is purple. Something about the yellow light bulbs and the peculiar shadows they make against the wallpaper. There are splashes down the side from a struggle. The way the water pours out over the edges, it could well be a hand reaching out to me. Inside the tub, she's already dead. Her eyes are wide-open underwater. I close them and briefly wonder if eyelids can hold fingerprints.

You've taken care of it.

The birds aren't in their cages. All the more reason to make it look like a suicide, the ceremony of a goodbye. On paper, her reaction would make sense after news of her father's death, even though I know she hated him deeply. It is the disappearing hour, not where I hide photos of us together, but where I tuck your wife in the silence of death, the backdrop of which will give us enough money to leave for years, for you to re-wed. Elsewhere, in Isfahan, where I hope they'll ask less questions.

If I let myself, I'd feel guilty for the women we have left or will leave behind. My mother, your aunt, your wife. I won't dwell on the thought. Momentum won't let me pause. I only have the capacity for our own gain.

Before I leave Mahtob's body, I scatter a few sleeping pills on the bathroom floor. It's like a game of finishing each other's sentences. You got rid of your wife, and I added the small detail to make it look less like murder and more like a suicide.

I stop at the door on my way out. Her long black veil asks to come with me, so I take it from the coat rack. I'll meet you on the third day of the third week of the new year.

35

It's emotional tinnitus. For a minute, I feel a sharp, unbearable feeling of guilt, a gong smack that reverberates for one brilliant, final lap before the nothingness. It happens when I think about Mahtob. I feel it, so much of it, then return to apathy. A hard arrow tears into my ribs when I think about Sumac. After that pain, when the episode ends, I feel nothing. I accept what has happened as something over, out of reach.

I am left with a worry. When the bandages are off, how will it feel? Not my body, which may or may not be prone to slouching depending on where I feel the redistribution of weight. What will happen to our love when it isn't a secret? We won't be able to kiss passionately in public, but we wouldn't, even if it was allowed. Not our style. I might prefer keeping our relationship a secret. For me, the transition is to ward off death, not to become a couple that taps love letters on each other's palms. We won't be new people. We'll be safer.

I think of the first fly that catches a whiff of fresh shit. Soon others hop through the same mess. Similarly, the cops are around Mahtob's body now. Maybe a car at first, joined later by others rubbing together their dirty palms. There is little sympathy for suicide, especially for a dead man's only daughter. Who will plan his funeral now? So selfish, trying to eclipse his death with her own.

I almost hear the conversations of cops circling around your apartment building, asking questions about your whereabouts because on the same day both your wife and your father-in-law died. Your attack might have saved you. You can explain leaving town for some reconstructive surgery to your jaw. Also, being attacked by a group of men could prove your gentleness. Couldn't fight back then, so what would make them think you could kill?

I wonder how Kaveh will react when he finds out Mahtob is dead. I scratch my eyes not as an admission of guilt but because a mosquito bit me near the duct. By the time it heals, by the time it itches less, I'll be closer to my next life. Not a new life, but the next one.

For the day, I worry a detective will be at my door to ask questions about you.

For a week, I eat yogurt off a paper plate facing the wall in our apartment. I can't bring myself to swallow anything too solid. My stomach is upset from some bug, I tell myself, not from guilt.

Before the month is over, before the final forty days following your wife's death, I visit the cemetery again. I lie down on a small section of grass and overhear people complain about the cost of rent going up, specifically the cost of paying for a grave.

"It's not like they can evict you," a woman says to another. Both are here to remember someone long dead, not a grave marked with fresh tears.

"You never know what money will make people do."

I visit my grandmother's plot one last time. I can come back to see her if I want, but not until our new life has solidified. Maybe I'll find work in Isfahan, cleaning out wastebaskets in our favorite hotel. Or I can become the ghost that haunts the local library as a tribute to my mother. I wash my grandmother's grave with a water bottle. I forget to save some at the tail end of the bottle to rinse my own hands, so I wipe the dirt on my pants. The soot reminds me of Omid. Maybe he's finished that charcoal drawing of me.

If circumstances were different, Mahtob would have met Kaveh before marrying you. And years from now, after a gentler death, one of her grandchildren would clean her grave.

My goodbyes take place quietly. I know I won't be back to this part of Tehran. Not for a time.

My mother isn't on the bottom floor of the central library. In case she makes it down there and chooses the same stacks to sit between, I've pulled out one book in particular. Not a symbolic one, detailing the voyages of river snakes. I simply flip a book over so the spine faces in. While reading or performing some recitation, she might look over at the book facing a different direction from the rest. If she adjusts the book, it'll be the closest to touching hands again.

36

For now, I look feminine enough. The pills have done a decent amount of work. I can't sleep flat on my stomach like I used to. We're months into the waiting game, until we reunite. I'm on the cusp of change. Come spring I'll be ready to leap.

I'm distracted by our old meeting places, even though we need to stay apart. We aren't seated on the steps or near the pavilion of flags. You never liked coming to Narmak. The last time we went, you stopped to talk to a man peddling tangerines in a wagon.

"King Tut's gold," he called them. But you were more interested in the blue fabric he used to cover the fruit from the sun. "All the sheep that year gave blue milk," the man said of the textile. We weren't sure what he meant, since his Afghani accent was too heavy.

My uncle's apartment feels safe again. I appreciate my neighbors. They still keep out of sight. When I get home from buying a new coat, I spot a boy at my door. From behind I can see his breath. He pants from a long bike ride in this weather, too cold for snow. The boy tucks a rolled up paper between the knob and the lock. The courier is about nine years old. Judging from his banged-up helmet, he's been making deliveries for most of his childhood.

"How'd you get in the building?" I ask.

He isn't startled.

"The gate wasn't closed all the way."

There are other papers in the kid's satchel, architectural plans and graphic design folios. I'm just one stop on his delivery route.

"Do people tip?" I ask.

"I can't tell you how to live your life."

He's not interested in small talk. I accidentally drop the coins I mean to hand to him. He puts his shoe over one that's about to roll away. I wait for the kid to leave before I unfurl the paper. I don't have time to ask him who sent it. He wouldn't know anyway. "What can I tell ya? Just one of my stops."

You've sent me a love letter. A low-quality lobby card from a 1940s American film. A woman stands behind a man with one hand grabbing his suit lapel. I can't quite remember the plot. A suitcase of money, a dead husband.

I put away all the groceries I bought, enough for two out of habit. Growing up, we'd split baklava to swallow far deeper than each other's tongues. And if ever I was depressed or anxious or overwhelmed, about us, about my mother, father, brother, or own ambivalent path, you'd say: "Focus on what you swallow, not what swallows you."

Remembering those confections works better than any incantation. They are inedible, all memories are, but they bring you here. There is love between us. I have proof in all the phantom sweets that coat my throat with phlegm from falling asleep without scraping them off my tongue.

Just then I remember the name of the film. The lobby card the boy left at our door.

Too Late for Tears.

37

The change was supposed to give us privacy. Now that it's over, I worry it has put me on further display. Sitting upright was an early nuisance, testing my poise with the shrill bursts below. My nerve endings begged themselves to heal. The bruises have become vague pains, like struggling to point to where exactly melancholia hurts. Somewhere.

How does one return the body to the sensual? After tedious conversations about genitalia, I want to be neither a wound nor a bleeding shrine. I kept to myself the marbled gleam of blood and discharge down my leg. Let me soften my body with myth. I now understand Leyli's classic Hollywood wigs. Better to discuss Garbo than to talk about dilating and douching to keep clean. I'd settle for references to Diroste, the mythical princess who sat in a white dome under Venus detailing the trials of love.

Let them say Anjir raised a finger and proclaimed: I am a woman now. And it was done. No one needs to know the surgical specifics.

I've rehearsed what I'll say when we reunite. "I couldn't love you as a man, even though I didn't mind being one." I'll probably forget my lines on the spot. Knowing my luck, you won't even come. Knowing my luck, you're dead or can't get it up for me as a woman. The third day of the third week of the new year. Perhaps you're already here in Isfahan, nearly three hundred miles from where we first called home.

I arrive at the labyrinthine hotel, our usual spot, during a blackout. I prefer the darkness, since it's my first time back as a woman. I hope nobody recognizes me. The staff tries to be extra accommodating because of the blackout. They smile even while balancing flashlights in their mouths and drag my bags to the elevator.

"We don't usually have this issue."

A lie. In our seven visits, always the same. Probably a weekly ploy to save electricity. I still prefer this hotel in Isfahan to the one my uncle owns in Tehran. Here, they light candles throughout, ones that never stay lit because of the steady breeze. As a result, the whole place smells like smoke from the ongoing relighting of tapers. Each hall flickers as guests navigate their way to their rooms, some with their phones and others with ultrabright flashlights provided by the staff.

The lobby is marked by a flood from years back. Three inches from the tiles, the lotus wallpaper is stained. Mud from the original walls peeks through. We knew this hotel was ours because of the vast, rectangular garden with enough hedges to make a labyrinth. The garden was once a ball-room. After the revolution, they cracked the ceiling to let air through. It's the main draw of the hotel, which makes it easier to overlook the ridiculous narrowness of the rooms.

The corner suites can barely fit a bed. But the true charm is the garden, even though we stay indoors to fuck.

People sit outside in banquet chairs to hear a speaker read poems by Omar Khayyam. Men in tuxedos and women in fancy dresses nod under tasseled umbrellas with moth holes. The exact same pattern, Ursa Major, dots each. The poets all look so tense in candlelight with their folded hands on their laps. Even the metallic fronds in corner niches yawn.

We used roses as our made-up slang. Too many roses. Too many fags. We usually made the joke in places we wanted to leave, a restaurant, a party, a street corner that was too crowded. It would also make sense here.

"Too many roses. Shall we go?"

"Excuse me." A woman taps me on the shoulder.

Since we've made this hotel our usual meeting place, our visits have aligned with a few others. Most of them keep their space. But not this American woman, who we call the Contortionist because of the way she bends to fit into any conversation. She's invited herself into our room more than once. She insisted on eating only her canned goods (peas) when I offered her a dolma. She has a bandage over her nose this time.

I look into her eyes and pause. A new game: worrying if strangers will recognize who I was. And will they react? She looks for a hint of recognition.

"I'm sorry," she says. "I thought you were someone else."

A sharp pain knocks me over, like when I was a cathedral buttressed with prosthetics to hold up what so badly wanted to collapse. I grit my teeth and clutch my thigh. I've stopped taking painkillers because I thought it was time to wean myself off of them. My scars have softened into what I pretend is dark pink moss.

She leans close and whispers to keep from drawing attention. "Are you all right?"

"It's the surgery," I say before I can stop myself.

"Oh, you had surgery too? What for?"

"You tell me yours and I'll tell you mine."

She avoids scratching her nose job until I leave the lobby.

The bellboy guides me to my room past cherubim fountains that sputter. The keys cause each keyhole to spew rust. Black stains the mouth of every doorknob. The coat rack in the corner of our room is purely decorative. The way the hooks are angled, all my clothes fall off. Even the oil lamps are for appearances only, as are the fireplaces snuffed with cement. I clear space in a drawer that's full of candlesticks molded with fish scales. The room divider is painted with ornate coral. This hotel is obsessed with the sea. Aquatic topiaries, nymph draperies, and conch-curl balustrades.

At the far end of my room, there is a mirror with five panels. Aside from the largest center rectangle, each side has two more panels tilting inward to make the reflection repeat infinitely. Each mirror pane is a slightly different color. The centermost is bluish, while the ones on the left and on the right vary from purple to puce.

I hiss at the various sites of pain on my body. Leyli might look at herself with pleasure now, with the bruises healed and the stitches no longer vying for attention. At least I'm done with the out-of-sync blinking that came from anesthesia. The jewel tones of my reflection distract me, not because I recognize myself and not because I don't. The iterations of my face flatten. It may seem impossible to separate the body from its history, but it is the accumulation of time, the ravages of age, the bruises peeled from the knee I see in the mirror, not with sadness, but acceptance that I am the sum of all the changes I have allowed and the ones that have been foisted on me.

"Hello, stranger," you'll say when you arrive. Tears will edge your eyes.

You will come. We will pretend nothing has happened.

You won't come. I'll pretend nothing has happened. I'll leave.

"Why not meet on an island?" the mirror asks. "At least there you could have swum together as two men, instead of being condemned to separate beaches for men and women."

Because like Tiresias, I needed the possibility of leaving and coming back. Not to my body as it was, but to where I was born, where my mother lived, where I first dreamt of us being together as husband and wife before I knew the words, the curses, the drafts of our goodbyes, before I knew piano benches could give splinters to my thighs. It is better, it is different. The blood we've spilled will forever connect our lips. We were vicious because of circumstance.

The mirror shakes its head. "You were vicious because you were vicious people."

No. Not anymore. There is a change reserved for rose martyrs. Brutality is behind us.

During the blackout, hotel workers set gabbehs in the garden for those who don't get a cross breeze in their room. It's too dark to even sleep. I wander the hallways down into the former library. In the corner, a magenta flicker catches my eye, not unlike a hidden cavern behind an ice cream shop. A jukebox emptied of its display sits against the southern wall. The top portion is blank, where CDs and track listings used to be. But the light inside still makes the plastic glow for some reason, even though the rest of the hotel is dark.

"An antique," the hotel proprietor says to a guest who sizes up the machine. "On its own circuit. It only takes American dimes. Just type in any combination of letters and numbers one through thirty-three to play Presley or Delkash. It's still a surprise to us all. Can't keep track of the songs hidden in this thing."

When the hotel lights flicker on again, I decide to eat before it gets too late. I plan to have dinner alone in my hotel room. The phone number for guest services isn't working. The busy signal always sounds faster on a hotel line. I head downstairs, where the receptionist is busy checking in three parties at once.

I circle the labyrinthine garden until I think I see your wife. I made a habit of spotting her from the periphery of your building, from downstairs, from across the street. I slept outside and found ways to go even closer. It isn't her at all. She's dead. Or perhaps Sumac is here too, or Omid comparing socks while standing guard of paintings locked in the basement, much like I stand guard over who we were. Will I have to re-edit all our memories now? A boy and a girl holding fruit while climbing the cliffs? No. We can start anew. The calmness combs the knots out of my hair with barely a touch.

Behind me I feel someone's breath. Mint. A mint kiss, mouths widened, feeling the body own and disown its warmth. Remember the garden Scheherazade spoke of where the people gave flowers for poems? We've earned a whole menagerie of damask roses colored from blood to carnelian.

I turn around. You and I meet again.

"Hello, stranger."

"Strange hello."

38

I tighten my veil. You circle. A sprig of mint in your coat pocket. Your hands, they look the same. You're taller, I think. I look closely to read your reaction, if you'll squint when you see me as a woman. A stern shock. Or a quiet disappointment. You respond with neither. The armistice is in place.

There are so many ways I can react. I can make a scene. But all conversations are a sort of scene. I can make a spectacle. But all interactions could suffer the spectacular with little effort. I let there be meaning in every gesture. The center of etiquette is hiding the ache.

"I thought you looked familiar," you whisper in my ear.

There is extra weight in everything we say.

"Where do we go from here?" I ask. You know what I mean, but play dumb.

"Dinner." There's only so much we can talk about in public. Perhaps it's better this way. You smile. "You're here. I'm here. We made it." Our plan worked. However messy. However clean. "I'll get us a room."

"I already have one."

"Then we'll have two." You hand me violets already in a plastic vase. We will speak nothing of the violence, of that pink hole in which we fell.

Mongolian tourists check in before you. I wait by the internet café. You're a sort of politician at the front desk, shaking hands and straightening your tie in perfect intervals. I remember teaching you how to tie a tie, and helping take it off.

"Have you changed all the way?" you ask in the elevator. Now everything has a triple meaning. That is how I know something is on the cusp.

"Have I?"

You take out a ring missing a stone. "It made me think of you."

The elevator door opens and I drop the ring when two men step in. Out of habit we separate to respective corners. One man takes a prolonged sniff and says nothing. He disapproves. He shakes his head like I'm a whore in ermine fur with miniver around my neck. He exhales like I'm pushed into his lungs.

"Too much perfume," he mumbles.

I'm not wearing any perfume, but it doesn't matter to him.

39

We have breakfast in my room, not yours. With a wave I refuse a bowl of melon; seeing it gored makes me feel faint. I sit on the corner of the bed and look out the window. Our electric kettle takes time to heat. The lid lights up. You hold a cup out to me. I slide it back. I'll only read one from which we both drink. We can play backgammon or watch a dubbed film like we did before our escape, before we knocked down lover pears that swung too closely to each other on a tree. We can burn our palms so others can't make sense of our lines.

"The kettle is state of the art," you say of the one you brought. "I got it in Thailand."

"Is that where you were?"

"Can't you tell?" You show off an even newer set of teeth, clean but worthless.

You put your hand on my neck. I flinch before I can train myself to sit still. You don't know what to say. I ask questions to disrupt the silence.

Where were you last Tuesday?

You can't remember. "I was somewhere thinking I'd meet my man."

I want to ask you to clarify. Maybe you have another man.

"My one and only." You put your hand on my lap. I pull away.

"What time did your flight take off?"

"3:05 P.M."

Do you still want to sleep with me? I don't know if I'd let you in just yet.

You flip through souvenir postcards I bought at the airport. They distracted me when I considered turning around because I imagined the pain of getting fucked for the first time. I remembered I had nowhere else to go. You stop on a postcard of Tabriz. In some sense, I'm a virgin again. We haven't even kissed. Not like we did when we were children sleeping on a rooftop with mosquito nets as bedsheets. Not like the accidental kiss when we shared a pillow.

You put an unlit cigarette to your mouth. "I don't want to pressure you to do anything."

Somehow, you've changed as well. Whereas before, you'd laugh, start on top of me, and there'd be this understanding, this pact of silence where we didn't say anything until the act was over and we'd sweated out our daily guilt. But now, change. Decorum. There isn't a beastly triumph in the conversation.

"My brother."

Your body tenses up. "What about him?"

"Was he one of the men?"

"From the attack?" You nod. "I thought I deserved it at the time. I was ashamed I was with someone else. Not you."

"You think that would have stopped him?"

While lifting a suitcase, my breast cracks at the stitch. "Don't panic." You fish out some bandages for me.

"Damn surgeon. Should have known he'd do a rush job just to get paid sooner."

"Don't worry. It's like your heart is bleeding."

I smile. "I don't keep my heart in my tit." I take a few Band-Aids. It doesn't stop our conversation. Seeing me in pain makes you nostalgic.

"We've always had a secret language of gesture," you say. "I know when you turn your head a certain way, I've made you nervous. And you know when I touch the underside of your chin, it means I want to be kissed. We understand each other."

I don't know what to do with your earnestness. I change the subject because I can't think of anything else to say.

"I met your wife's lover."

You pull back. "Sure." You think I'm trading a joke for a joke.

"I might have turned him." You realize I'm not kidding. "What?"

"He wasn't very gentle after we kissed."

You stand up to excuse yourself as if you thought we'd have no more animosity between us. "If you aren't a vahshi in furs, I don't know who is." It stings. I throb between who we were and who I hope we will become. Perhaps I will always be a brute.

After you leave, the lights go out again. All the hotel guests let out a moan. I sit at the beveled mirror. A diagonal light comes in through the window. I sit so it slashes my neck. Shadows wait patiently before they emerge from the walls. On the bed, I picture past fucks on the satin. The travesties pucker before they disappear. I run my cheek over the violets in the plastic vase for some contact.

I open your suitcase and take out a few toiletries. I only own counterfeit luggage. Yours are lined with real leather and silk. I finish a bottle of plum soda and open a book from your suitcase. A pop-up book with a holy mountain, a mosque, a temple. In my haste, I knock over the bottle of cola and watch a cathedral fizz as it seeps.

You don't come back for hours. I worry I've scared you off again. To another man? Back to your wife's grave?

I call your cell phone. No answer. With you gone, I sit in the taloned tub. Best to bathe with an open mouth, so I can swallow my own blood and filth.

Leyli answers after one ring.

"Rose tea with rock candy," she insists over the phone. "It'll help with the nausea."

She doesn't ask bullshit pleasantries about my trip to Isfahan, flight meals and airport magazines bent open from those who read but don't buy.

"How's my mother?" I ask her.

"She's fine. Eats everything, except baghali polo." She turns to my mom. "Lady, I slaved for hours picking through fresh dill." I hear them both laugh in a way my mother and I never could. Leyli puts the receiver back to her face. "Is Zal there?"

"Yes."

"And is every moment a movie scene?"

"Yes, but I don't know what kind."

"You're not going to find suitcases of money. It's probably all hidden safely in his bank account."

"I'm sure."

I look down at my wrist. Have I shrunken too? I realize I'm comparing myself to a different telephone receiver, the one I'm used to in my uncle's apartment.

"You deserve the best from love." Her concern is motherly.

I wait for you in the hotel library. I sit by the jukebox to see if anyone has an American dime. It might be time to finish the conversation with you in my head, but it's a ribbon, an arabesque I can't yet end. I stick my head out the library window, the sill as my pillow, and try to forget the memory of teeth.

"Here," a hotel employee says as he passes.

He flips me a coin I push into the jukebox. I take my guess at numbers, since the display is blank. After a brief pause, the mechanisms shake themselves awake. Magenta lights resurrect the machine. A song begins. The call to prayer plays on the Victrola. The vinyl sat so long on an Ellington, imprinted on the surah is the slight sigh of a dirge, a funerary fade for the love of the love-me-nots. For us, there is not enough pomp. Never, really.

40

I can't remember what brand the samovar was. I'd like to find the same one made of brass in the shopping plaza. I need something to mail to Leyli, because I owe her. A samovar so that when I visit, I can read her fortune with the ulterior motive of hearing her tell her life story. She will appreciate an appliance with an extra-long cord, depending on which hotels she visits on her travels.

At the entryway of the mall, a homeless man bites the ear off a Mickey Mouse popsicle. I use a different entrance than the last time I came. Other women fan themselves. Can they tell I was once a man by the way I take off my shoes to take out a rock? By how I carry myself under the veil? But I see others with even less grace. They nod their heads. A word, nothing more. But I feel them watching me. Are my socks too thin? My toenails too rough? My nose too uneven?

I came to this side of Isfahan with my grandmother once. By then chemo had softened her brain. We got to a mosque and separated with fellow men and women. After, we shared a glass of watermelon juice and she kept on about how hard it must be to make such a drink. I scribbled a note on a napkin to buy her a blender. She died before I came across that note again.

At the shopping plaza, a man shakes the beaded pillow-cases in the window of his furniture store. The flash from a passport photo studio grabs my attention. This keeps me from recognizing the American woman from our hotel. She pulls my arm and accidentally jams her three shopping bags into me.

"Dear!" She lunges for a hug. "Anjir, this time I'm sure it's you." The gauze on her nose scrapes my face in another awkward hug. I pull back. I wonder if she ever looks in the mirror at her nude body and thinks, "Is this it?"

I'm worried she'll ask me specific questions about why I've transitioned. "I'm looking for a samovar."

"I saw some on the other side." She grabs my hand and pulls me to the escalator.

"I'm looking for a specific one."

We pass a cookery shop, and one that only sells baby clothes. She slows to feel a panther skin on display in a mall kiosk, then charges forth.

"Is this one fine?" She points to a small corner shop filled with night-lights and LEGOs. She's misunderstood what I said, but I don't let on.

We drink strawberry smoothies, her treat, in the food court. Unripe fruit, the juice is gray. I don't know what to say to her. She reaches for my hand under the table. Even without eye contact, I feel I'm the floor show.

Talking to the American about you would ruin it. You're mine. To put it into words, to mutilate it into an affair that fits into tidy sentences would devastate me somehow. I could blame meds for making me extra sensitive, but I know it's deeper. On one hand, I've never been good at summing up my emotions. A sigh and a grunt say plenty. A laugh, a furrowed lip. But simple paragraphs are work. Sentences cheapen our secrets. How will I tell our story now that I'm forced to admit it? Man and woman. Eventually, husband and wife. Can't we be Anjir and Zal without having to over-explain? A deep, brutal pain. It'll pass. I won't feel this depth again.

A tear rolls down the American's straw when she considers what she thinks is our tale.

"Let me give you something," she says.

"I'm fine."

"Please." She digs in her bag, tosses out a few tissues. She hands me lip gloss. "Cantaloupe flavor. You'll love it."

I finish the smoothie, now warm. Her sweaty hands leave my wrists pink.

"What made you decide to change?" she asks.

"Hah." I laugh at the absurdity of her question, one without an easy answer.

Your laptop is on when I return to my hotel room. On the computer, a bootleg of an old Rita Hayworth movie plays. She taunts Orson Welles in a hall of mirrors. I minimize the window. There's a picture of me on your desktop. As I was. At Hafiz's temple where I whirled until I fell down.

I climb into bed and try to kiss you, but I realize you aren't there. Just your bunched up robe from some duty-free shop during your travels. I knew you before you memorized the names of casinos in Monaco or Las Vegas. I can name all the things that have ever given you nightmares. Car crashes, your father, and losing all your teeth. In that moment, it hits me. The thought makes me dizzy. I've been chasing your absence. Leaving could be as easy as leaving. Your aunt was right. Have you ever looked for me?

I dump the contents of the dresser into my suitcase, rolled shirts with the tags still on in case I died on the operating table. I even take what's in the wastebaskets. I won't leave any of it behind, not the cola bottles, the socks, the eyeliner shavings, though I sharpened a pencil I have no interest in using. There is a goodbye in every gesture.

Anything can be a memento. An orange rind on the windowsill. A dead fly next to the bedpost. A rose that died midgrowth. I can't stay behind for you or my mother or an earlier version of myself. From my bag, I grab your wife's veil. Black. With it on, I fade into the room, dark too at this hour. I prop open the door for light while standing at the beveled mirror.

I did it for you. No. I shouldn't have. The gods might ask if love is better as a man or as a woman. Either way, it cost me my sight because I didn't want to change, because

I was perfect in some way. But life is building a cake only to watch it fall.

A click. I know the sound. It's unmistakable. Behind me, a gun is cocked.

It's genius. I see your shape in the blue pane of the mirror. You close the door. Your outline leans against the window. From this angle, your gun would shoot right through my back. That wouldn't be dramatic enough for us. I position myself so the bullet would shatter the mirror and end my reflection.

"Is that why you brought me here?" I say without turning. "To get rid of both your lovers?"

"Not quite." It isn't your voice. Almost, but not quite.

Kaveh. Taller than before. Vice must have given him back his height. He points his gun. "You deserve as many bullets as a fig has seeds."

"But why?" I ask. "Because of Mahtob? I wasn't the one who got rid of her."

"Of course not." He grins. "I did." He can tell I'm confused. "Sweetheart, I wasn't fucking her. I was fucking him. I've been to your apartment before. I've been to your hotel room too. With Zal, without Zal." He laughs. "Now look at you. Your faggy voice is faggier. Your tits are barely worth looking at. And why'd he want you with a twat? That night. Before he was taken to the hospital, he was with me. He might have been caught with the kid later, but that was after. Two glasses. One condom wrapper, even though he fucked two different men that night."

Taper candles drip directly onto the table. They hiss along with his laughter. How sweetly he becomes mad. He stands midway through the narrow room where a bullet might ricochet against the walls and bounce back into his own neck. It's a chance he's willing to take.

"It's a wonder you're still alive," he says. "I hated you so much. My hate alone, more than any bullet, should've killed you. And yet."

You enter.

Zal, my love. You drop a blue fruit. A blue pomegranate. You panic at the sight.

"No!" you yell. "It was a mistake. Just one mistake after another."

Was it? Maybe you thought only betrayal would send me away. But somehow it only brought you closer to me.

Kaveh turns to you. "Who do you pick? Her or me?" It takes a moment for me to realize I'm the her in the ultimatum. Kaveh asks the question we both want answered. The silence lasts for too long. "Fine." Kaveh aims his gun at me. "I'll make the decision for you."

You run toward me. I open my arms to hide you in your wife's veil. Inside, we both hear the echo of nightingales from their years of keeping the fabric company. Kaveh fires three shots. Something about my veil confuses him. One bullet shatters the five-paneled mirror in the corner of the room. The bullet bounces across two panels. A third panel shatters from the impact. The bullet breaks the spell and the mirrors all turn colorless, not purple or gold or blue. I feel you slump in my arms. A bullet in your back.

Kaveh gasps at his own doing. He hears a noise behind him, the first stirrings in response to his rampage. He points the gun toward the hall and runs. A sweet kiss. His bullets write verses on the walls.

I weep over your face. My tears land on your eyes.

"Brazen girl," you say. "Brutal boy."

I shake you to keep you awake, anything for us to share another word. A kiss, three kisses. But the lights flicker on and off. In the veil, in the company of the sounds of nightingales long dead, I kiss you. My one love.

You put your hand on my cheek. "Tell me something that matters."

"Nothing. Nothing matters wildly."

You rub my cheek and smile. "Your beauty mark just came off."

I pull away, but you hold me tighter. "I figured you were the type that'd like a beauty mark, something exotic."

"I loved you before I was any type. I'd even like you as a bearded woman."

"Then stick around, mister. My beard itches like hell."

Our kiss hasn't tasted like mint in years. Now, blood. You without teeth or you with a pearl lodged in your intestine. I kiss you. I kiss you and roses sprout everywhere we've kissed, in the pink lake of Maharloo, outside the stone garden, and beside the carpet washer who wetted the end of his broom and brushed the threads. A kiss in the bookstore. A rose grows in all the squares, within the wind catchers of Aghazadeh. Roses shift beside the thousand colors of Nasir Al Mulk. The ruins laugh weeds out of their blemishes. And inside Pulvar River, the water ripples from rocks we haven't thrown. Full gardens grow beside the overchlorinated public pool that burns feet if they dangle without shoes. See where we stood in the cherry rain, named for its taste? I drank enough until I grew sick on bitterness. You kissed me to get me to stop. A single rose grows from the day we trespassed to see the Sultana eclipse. To hide, we swayed with the gravestones during the earthquake. Perhaps you are Zahak and I am your two snakes, me as a woman and me as a man. I pull away from our kiss. We don't turn to stone.

Without speaking, you respond. Goodbye, stranger. Strange goodbye.

Your search for blue ends in this room. Everything about us bleeds blue. All the roses in the corners. All the ashes of our burned photos. The killing jar. On my way downstairs for help, I pass circus performers in their suites. The snake charmer unfurls a heavy rope for her apprentice to practice with the weight of a cobra. I swear I see a crow on fire somersault in reverse. Kids will point to the charred mountains toward what was once a bird.

Our pomegranate plan. We were bound to bleed.

I remember asking once in our harlequinade, "Can you love me forever?"

Your response: I can until I can't. I will until I won't.

Acknowledgments

To my agent Mariah Stovall at Trellis Literary Management: you are my best case scenario. Thank you for embracing the horror and humor with me. On we go, subversive hand in hand. Katie Raissian, my guiding star, my khohar from a different mohdar, the Shohreh to my Googoosh: I adore you. You never flinched. Noir, mythology, cum? Let's ride. Grove Atlantic, you are my dream publisher. Your books have long populated my life even before I could afford bookshelves. Many thanks to Noah Grey Rosenzweig for the generous notes and feedback. Amy Hundley and Joseph Payne, thank you for welcoming the torch song into your lives. Special thanks to Allison Malecha, foreign rights agent extraordinaire, for getting the word out abroad. There should be a book club dedicated to your thoughtful emails. Thank you to the team at Le Bruit du monde in France, my UK coagent Florence Rees, and my UK editor Leonora Craig Cohen at Serpent's Tail. Sarah Gurcel, my French translator, your clarifying questions helped with the final embroideries. May we continue to discuss the quadruple entendres of seeds.

To my dear friends: Aidé Aceves (for friendship in a world of broken wishbones), Jennifer Silva, Stephanie Mejia, Jessie Furuta, Victoria Jaschob, Sarvi Chan, Bridgit King, and Kirby Lima. You are the air I come up for. Love to love you.

Thank you to the teachers: Mrs. Haddock, my second grade teacher, for encouraging me and for encouraging my parents to do the same; Mrs. Kennedy, who brought me the word quietude; Jaleh Pirnazar for breaking open Persian film history; Linda Williams for the melodrama; Russell Ferguson, for notes on an early, wretched draft. There's still some Pasolini in there.

To the women at every Barnes & Noble Writers Club meeting I went to from junior high through high school, thank you for taking me seriously. Whether I was writing greeting card–style poetry, or stories about sex work during the apocalypse, you were my confidants. I'm glad you felt comfortable reading your erotica in front of me.

Mom, Dad, Mehdi, and Banafsheh, thank you for your cautious encouragement. You took turns driving me to the aforementioned writers meetings, even if they took place during a Lakers game. What commitment! And you kept my life full of journals with golden edges, which gave the "believe" years their magic.

Thank you, Kristin Remington, for taking an interest in my creative world when I felt spent. You helped pick the creative scab that made way for fresh blood. Navid Najafi, name twin, thanks for helping me embrace the complexity, and for the Queen of Snakes. Stephanie Wolf, how did I end up with your friendship and support? Just lucky, I guess.

For those interested in further exploring the topics of this work, I recommend the writing of historian and theorist Afsaneh Najmabadi, and the documentary film *Be Like Others* by Tanaz Eshaghian.

Luis Carlos, my love, my favorite: thank you for your endless patience (jk). Thank you for the joy. You make every day feel like the best vaudeville routine. The fortune teller was wrong, that cockblocker.

Once during an argument about some of my racier writing, my mom said, "Think about your family!" With immense clarity, I am. This work is for my brethren: the queer and trans communities, the women of Iran and elsewhere, the beings just trying to live their lives, love their loves, and exist without constant fear of being murdered.

And to my dear cousin Bahareh, who died trying to leave Iran: I write this with extreme acknowledgment of the unfairness. We'll always have Darband.